ROMAIN DOLCY'S

Paradise
A Hidden Truth

Written by
Romain Dolcy

Titles by Romain Dolcy

Emotivations
The Verses of a Man
Paradise 'A Hidden Truth'
Paradise 'Everything's Eventual'
Paradise 'The Journey Continues'

Romain Dolcy's Paradise 'A Hidden Truth"

This book brought to you by CreateSpace Independent Publishing Platform / published by arrangement with
Romain Dolcy

ISBN: 978-1-4973-4182-1

This Book Printed in
The United States of America

PARADISE

A Hidden Truth

Prologue

In the Beginning

Racing against the times is something that many attempt but to no avail. Time has made a permanent and terrifying name, and has not once been defeated-by anyone or anything. A good example of her mark is the dinosaurs. Even when we think we are ahead of time or that we have accomplished; she shows her smiling face and proves us wrong. Her only friends are fate and reality. Reality can never be altered neither can fate; for whatever will be-will be.

For those select few who are spared by some intervention or other life changing or lifesaving event, or those who believe they have cheated death; you never did. It just wasn't your time, but just a few unstoppable moments later our true time comes. No one dies too early; we simply die when it's our time to go. Just remember one thing, life's a pre-planned event, everything we do or say already foretold. Though we are all given freewill, who's to say where destiny will lead us?

In the early times, things were different. Countless reports of possession, malice and mysterious disappearances were not unusual; they were an everyday occurrence. There were various accounts of demons walking the earth, families plagued and people falling ill with no diagnosis of known ailments, spells cast on individuals and witches wreaking havoc on innocent lives.

The existence of innocence marred by the reality that nobody is really innocent. You may not be guilty of something, but knowing anything about it, even hearsay or the most menial detail takes any innocence away. Some say innocence lies within a new-born, still we can't tell for sure the inner workings of the mind, especially that of a child or even a new-born. Until we have a complete and comprehensive understanding of the mind or brain, we can't give an accurate account or report on many things, including innocence.

Who is to speak of innocence? For in truth, nobody is really innocent. We may not recall everything that has occurred in life, be it your personal life or that of another perhaps even in what some may call an alternate life; being if you believe in reincarnation or past lives.

Whatever you do, remember this: Time always sings to her own tune, dances to her own beat and composes to her own rhythm. There are no alterations offered, no do-overs or remakes. Do all that you can in the here and now, because now is all that counts. The future becomes the now, the now becomes the past, and the past is history. Nothing lasts forever and forever does not last that long when it's gone.

Paradise: A Hidden Truth

1298 Bratislava, one stormy evening Emila, a young mother was home taking care of her three year old twins Edric and Edvina. Her husband Ulrich was due the following night from foraging and hunting. She was making porridge for her family on a three stone coal pot, her house dimly lit as she leaned over stirring her pot vivaciously; stirring and adding in her ground cornmeal and fresh goat milk. A dim candle light was timidly flickering in the common room, and then it became more aggressive; alarmed, she rushed over to her children playing in their wooden cradle. She held them in her arms and rushed to the bedroom; she hurdled in a corner and hugged them tightly to her.

She beckoned them to stay quiet. A loud pound was heard from the common room, the front door fell to the ground. An unnatural silence ravaged through the house. A dark semi-transparent cloaked figure drifted in, slowly making its way through the log cabin. The only sound that could be heard was absolute silence. The dark figure floated around, checking every room along its way.

"Stay quiet my angels, don't move..." Emila whispered to her children, hiding them under the bed. She ran to the chest at the foot of the bed pulling out a silver cross. She whispered a prayer clenching the cross tightly to her heart. Placing the string from the cross around her neck, she scurried to the doorway of the bedroom. Just at that very moment, the figure approached her, rushing sadistically.

"Give me the children at once!" It commanded in a stern distorted voice.

Fire covered the figure, blue and green flames. It attacked her; sending black flames at her, black glowing flames that resembled dragons. These were known as spurs. A spur was the fiery mark of a reaper, it was his weapon; a creature created by flames. As they near her, the dragons took form. She raised her arms and faced them toward the dragons.

"Lumen ad draconum," she shouted, "evanescant extemplo!"

The dragons dispersed leaving grey fragments of smoke. She raced toward the reaper, cross glowing in her hand. Now staring directly into its red hallowed eyes, she grabbed the cross, ready for combat.

"You are not welcome here Glatisvar! I know you are no spirit, you have no soul and this ground is blessed!" she shouted striking the figure through the heart with the silver cross.

A loud crack was heard like that of a whip and the sound returned. The figure vanished into thin air, a white orb of light remained. Fourteen small sparks of white light dispersed from the orb resembling tiny comets going in an anticlockwise direction after seven cycles they went to her silver cross. The cross glimmered then ceased. In the spot where Glatisvar hovered, a small silver coin fell to the ground.

"Anima illuminábit" she whispered, hanging the cross around her neck. She walked toward the coin, hand outstretched and the coin summoned to her hand.

"Veri et ex euentu" she read off the coin, heaving it into a small herb pouch tied around her waist.

She rushed over to the bed where she hid the twins, "It's time to leave my sweets". She inscribed a message on the headboard.

She packed a small bag of supplies, changes of clothes, food and all her books. "It's time to move again." She said flustered. She spun her right hand around, her palm facing up bringing her fingers in from her pinkie to her thumb, the bag disappeared. "Travel lightly..."

She also took her two cats along with her, Ginger a gold and white striped tabby and Maestro an all-black male. She set off on foot, walking toward the Village of Ra, a small town to the east. She put her babies in a woven chest carrier that wrapped around her neck and shoulders. She stretched her hand to the sky her fist balled, slowly outstretching her fingers and red lights expelled. She whispered her husband's name and the lights headed west.

She walked hastily, not stopping to rest. The babies were both asleep, cautious not to wake them. A bright radiant light morphing into a lady dressed in white appeared beside her. Someone had come to her aide. It was a pharus.

"Samira, it's happening again. They are back for the children."

"Emila my child... have no fear, for darkness cannot exist without light and the light without darkness."

"Samira, protect us!"

"Lucis ab ortu ad occasum vivit in tenebris, lucem tenebris est. Crepusculum adfert lucem matutinam, claudit die parit nocte. Lux vitam in noctem, in tenebris non die recessit."

A radiant beam surrounded them, so bright it was blinding. As quick as it came it vanished, along with Samira. Emila started off again walking even faster heading toward the east; she knew that at any moment more reapers would show or even worse, she feared that demons would be sent instead. They wanted her twins and would stop at nothing to get them. The one thing evil spirits could not harm were twins. If Lilith ever got hold of her twins, she'd become even more powerful. Harvesting them as sacrifices and using their parts to make a totem or their souls to feed to the devil in order to appease him. The only thing is they had to be caught by living beings as spirits; demons or devils couldn't touch twins. They were untouchable to anything undead or things that lived in the shadows... or anything from hell.

The reapers were the only ones who could because they were still humans; the only difference is that they had no souls; empty beings, vespers thirsting for gratification, no feelings of happiness, love or hope; just darkness and endless pain. They gave their souls to the evil sorceress Lilith the most powerful sorceress known in these parts, to gain their most wanted earthly desires. They longed for riches, and fame and immortality. Lilith used their souls to make her payment to the devil, enslaving them forever as her minions. No one knew her age, but they all feared her power. They were all frightened enough to bend to her will and every desire. No one ever dared to go against her; those who did all met untimely deaths or strange things happened to them and their families. The only group that had survived battles against her were the 'Portarent Lucis' or the Bringers of Light.

The silence had returned this time it was a searing silence even louder than the first, she knew this only meant that more reapers were near. She started running, a race to save her life, to save humanity. She entered into the thick woods, her woven carrier clung tightly to her body. Reapers materialised all around her.

"You there, give up the twins! Lilith demands that we take you back to her at once!" shouted one of the reapers.

"I will not, I know she wants my children. She will not have them!" she replied with noticeable fear in her voice, tears flowing down irrepressibly from her eyes.

"Don't even try using any of your powers aura, there are too many of us and only one of you."

At that moment, a spectrum of light manifested, just as quick as lightening it came and disappeared. With that something materialised but it all happened so fast. Just where the light emerged something began to form. The reapers had all halted, freely afloat in mid-air; they appeared to be withdrawing. Then the silhouette of the figure appeared, outlined in black but almost translucent. It was a lumen; protectors of the light. They were extremely powerful, possessed powers beyond imagination, but they were not as powerful as the pharus.

Levitating there above the ground was a dark skinned man in a luminescent silvery white cloak. His face could not be seen, but he descended majestically toward the ground. He spun around clockwise; all the reapers began dispelling spurs at him. Dragons, snakes, lions, scorpions and other beasts hurled toward him. He was engulfed, covered by a spartacum. A spartacum was what formed when all the spurs came together creating what resembled a fire demon.

"Get her! The spartacum won't last long! Xavier is strong!" shouted one of the reapers.

They all rushed toward Emila. She tried to escape but there was nowhere to run to, she was surrounded. She used her powers but they had no effect against all the reapers. They neared her, taunting words and laughing. They took hold of her arms, holding her like a prisoner.

While taking her captive, they didn't realise Xavier had broken free. He used their own spartacum as a distraction. He had them all in one place, now was the time to attack. He waved his hand toward where the reapers held Emila; as he did bales of hay fell to the ground with a white dress.

"We've been tricked!" yelled one of the reapers. "Retreat!"

Xavier laughed; he knew that Emila and the twins were taken back to their secret place, Terra Lucis by Samira. "Elucido! Anima illuminábit." With that, light consumed the reapers.

The battle between the light and the darkness had been going on for centuries. No one knew when it began, but it was sure that the end was nowhere in sight. Nothing exists without its opposite, for there would be no balance. A break in the equilibrium could mean the end for all that we know. Everything comes to an end eventually… That is anything that has a start. Time has no start and it has no finish, it is constant and continual. Time was there before there ever was a beginning because the beginning was marked by time and it will remain long after there is an end. The

only thing that can defeat the inevitable is the inevitable itself.
Time waits for no man, so why wait for time?

Chapter 1

Small Land Big Secrets

I grew up in the village of Paradise Falls, a small agricultural and fishing community on the eastern coast of Isla de Tesoro. Isla de Tesoro or Eve (of the West) as the locals called her was a very small island known mostly for her rolling hills and mountains as well as her extensive history. The island which was rich due to her volcanic nature wasn't only beautiful, it emanated mystery. Legends said that there were diamond farms as well as other minerals such as gems, rubies and emeralds that could be mined, harvested and cultivated. The island had been fought for over centuries and had changed hands a recorded eighty-five times since it was first fought for, more than anywhere else on earth.

From the Germans, Spaniards, Russians, Dutch, British and French, the culture was very rich and quite diverse. There were all kinds of activities and events and holidays in place to celebrate our fair nation's extensive history; a lot of which had been left out and forgotten over the years as the newer generations replaced the true Tesoros or Everets as they were nicknamed. As the island became more populated, things changed.

Eve was a nation very strong in the Catholic faith and upbringing; bordered on the east coast by the Atlantic Ocean and on the west coast by the Caribbean Sea. It was just a rare precious gem, a treasure tucked away directly in the middle of the archipelago. Her geographical location bore no surprise as to why she was so sought after. What fuelled our community economically was primarily agriculture, particularly lobster, crab, shrimp and octopus fishing, and banana farming. That was our mainstay, what really kept us together. Due to her volcanic nature, her grounds mothered fertile soils which made farming easier. Eve truly and easily owned the title 'Lush Country', for she was truly lush in all senses of the word.

There were four main schools in Paradise Falls, the Paradise Falls Community Preschool which was basically a day-care but they taught kids the basics like reading and writing, as well as addition and subtraction up till the age of four, where they moved on up to the Paradise Falls Roman Catholic Infant school. At the Infant School it was from age four to eight. Then there were the Paradise Falls Primary School and the Paradise Falls Secondary School, which was like junior high and high school.

I don't remember much before the age of four, but what I do remember is growing up I was always seen as different and weird. I was never fascinated by playing with toys or running outside though I was very active, I spent most of my time reading. Television never intrigued me, unless it was some science fiction program, something about space or aliens, or nature programs. I was locked on to the National Geographic hour, because at that time we only had three channels in Paradise. Not much to look forward to, unless they had some horror film or perhaps something by the great Stephen King.

Paradise: A Hidden Truth

At school I started reading from the age of four and by the time I was five I was at an advanced reading level, by then I was already writing poems, essays and short stories. Very strange things would happen, things I didn't quite understand. These things were what really led to my interest in researching, history and anything considered as bizarre, paranormal or supernatural. The first time I saw something that I can remember, I was four years old. Drinking my bottle as I walked with my cousin Trisha to my grandmother's house, I heard strange voices coming from my grandmother's roof. It was apparent that Trisha didn't hear what I did because I pointed and she just pointed with me and started singing nursery rhymes: Twinkle, Twinkle.

The more I looked to where the sound came from, the louder it became. I heard footsteps and walking and grumbling. She said that she heard a frog hopping and croaking. At that moment, I saw a naked man resembling a frog jumping from the roof; it seemed as if he was shedding his outer layer, his frog skin. He got stuck in the neighbours' fence, I saw as he changed completely back to human form. My cousin never noticed, I yanked and tugged on her shirt until she looked. Exasperatedly astonished she ran over to the block iron fence to try to assist him.

"Mr. Graham, what are you doing here this early? Where are your clothes?"

"I was only looking for my hat", he replied "a strong wind blew it this way, I was only trying to get it back."

"How did you manage to get stuck in the fence?"

He stayed silent for a while, looking around; tongue slowly retracting. His eyes fell directly on me, he looked angry, staring at me intently a tone of rage in his beady eyes... "Get that thing away from me!" He started yelling and screaming as he pointed in my direction.

Soon the other neighbours heard the hubbub; they all came out of their houses to see what all the commotion was over. My parents rushed over to the spot where we stood. My mother grabbed me and took me inside my grandmother's house. My cousin stood in the same spot, petrified. Strange things like this were not new to the people of Paradise, but they were all great pretenders. Stories like this spread across the country and were cast off as just stories.

There were nights when I had dreams so real that the following morning I would wake up with scratches and bruises. It got to the point where I even found water on my person or dirt or blood according to what I dreamt that night. These dreams felt like they were meant to harm me. I told my parents whose initial idea was to take me to relate what I remembered to the parish priest. From that point on I would write as much as I remembered, I'd even draw pictures and anytime something out of the ordinary had taken place, I would head down to the presbytery to report it.

One time a teacher of mine Pearl Owens found one of my drawings with what I remembered from my dream, she created a spectacle and took me to the school counsellor, Alecia Watts. They insisted that I undergo treatment for my 'condition' as if I were diseased. They said I was traumatized and needed to partake in more children's activities. I was removed from all competitions and all boards including the Matheletes which at that time was my favourite group. I was devastated; I was determined to have my revenge. Every counselling session I behaved like I didn't know why I was there and seeing I was labelled as crazy and disturbed, I played along and played my part well. When Father Monroe caught air of what had been taking place, he pulled me out of counselling and made sure he let them know that if they tried any funny business like that he would take it to the extreme. He let it be known that science would never be able to solve or explain everything in life neither would it decipher all or life's mysteries, for science came after many things and it was not perfect.

My parents were never contacted by the school to be informed of any of these proceedings and I never told them. It seemed like the counsellor and my teacher were conspiring to overthrow Father Monroe and have me institutionalised. They went beyond their means to do all in their power while Father Monroe a lot wiser had contacted my parents and all personnel who needed to be notified. My parents were furious; they'd always been overprotective and sensitive when it came to their family, especially their children as any sensible parent would. My father being a member of the Ministry of Education and my mother a nurse took every measure to make certain that the situation was rectified. I can say that many jobs were lost and vacant, including that of Alecia and Pearl.

I saw other things growing up, but one thing in particular seemed to haunt me even into adult life that I could never shake off. It never frightened me, but it did make me uncomfortable that no one else saw it but me. It stood about three feet tall, though it seemed to be in a sitting stoop. Its body was hunched over; skin a scaly tone, brown colour, appeared black with sharp red areas. It never moved, never looked my way. It just sat in silence. For years I thought it was my imagination or perhaps even my conscience but that changed at the age of fifteen, when something different happened, it stare at me directly into my eyes.

Emptiness was the feeling that swept over me, dark and barren as if it bore no soul, no heart, no life, just darkness. Chills run through me, why was my imagination so convincingly livid? The only thing that was on my mind at that point was getting out of the house, as far away from this thing as I could. This creature that had plagued me silently and dismissingly for years and finally it acknowledged me; it let me know it was there just as I was. My first thought was to head down to the church and let the priest know what had happened. Describing it to him, an expression of dread appeared on his face. He immediately called my mother who was there within minutes. With apprehension and trepidation he reached for a book in a locked cabinet and began to explain what was happening to me. For the first time he showed me a picture of the creature. It was exactly the same as what I had been seeing. He also said that this book was only taken out in extreme situations and had never been shown to anyone who had not been ordained but explained to me that this was an extremely rare case.

Evil was out to get me and they wanted me dead. My protection lay in my birth and I could not be harmed as they wanted. He explained that perhaps the conception process until my birth held ultimate protection against evil. I knew nothing about my birth that was out of the ordinary at that time. The most I knew is that I was born a month earlier than my due date and there were many complications, which cause me to spend my first few weeks in an incubator. I wondered why anything would want me dead. I didn't think I crossed anyone that terribly and why were demons of death out to get me? It was too much to take in all at once. My mother didn't say much about it, she just ensured that I did as Father Monroe instructed. She also did her part, from then on up until the day I was ready to ship off to university... she still does up to this day.

August was quickly upon us, the University of Maine had been calling my name. In just a few more days it was time to bid Paradise adieu, to make acquaintance with a new distant land. Away from my family for ten years, in my mind it sounded like a lifetime. The day I left Paradise I thought would be the end of all the weird happenings. I was convinced that change was eminent and all these bizarre and supernatural encounters were a thing of the past and would remain there, but nothing can exist in complete darkness.

Friday the thirteenth of August 1999, was the day I left Paradise. It was bittersweet, the beginning of new chapters in my new life. My future was becoming my present and my present was becoming my past. Uncanny how life worked out, but I was ready to face the challenges. No one else but myself could achieve my dreams for me. It was time to face the world, time to grow up and spread my wings without my nurturing nest close by.

Chapter 2

Nothing Changed

After a two hour layover in Atlanta and another one hour at La Guardia, I finally got to Bangor International at two the following morning on August fourteenth. I was greeted by my Uncle Earl and Aunt Lucinda, Trisha's parents. Aunt Lucy was my mother's first sister. Though all my mother's siblings resembled my grandparents, Aunt Lucy and mom were usually mistaken for each other from childhood even to this day. Growing up we always heard the stories of their adventures. They were so horrid; they got the title around town as 'the trouble makers from the hillside'. She and my mother had always been close though my mom was ten years younger they shared the same personality. I always thought they were identical twins. They even thought the same way.

The ride back to the house lasted about thirty minutes; time spent catching up and sharing stories and laughs. I enjoyed family time; it made life so much more meaningful. Having loved ones around, people who cared, who shared embarrassing stories from your youth as well as theirs. As we drove I looked around just taking in the scenery. Maine was beautiful, it reminded me of home though it was a bit more modernised, the buildings and roads definitely said we were no longer in Tesoro. As we drove on and shared laughs and stories, nostalgia started to kick in. Nature was all over, it almost felt like home.

I gazed over and just then in a vehicle driving alongside us, I saw it again. The creature, hunched over in its usual position. The windows of the car alongside us froze over. I tried to look away, but my mind wondered; this thing followed me, just as a shadow would… it latched onto me. Slowly it raised its head and turned to face me. Its eyes slowly opened; there was nothing but darkness, emptiness. Leaning slowly toward the window its focus on me, then it vanished leaving behind a wisp of smoke. I blinked my eyes and shook my head lightly and all that remained was a family smiling and waving at us. More and more this thing, this demon was becoming more relentless at letting its presence be known. It was becoming bolder, and a lot more forceful.

We pulled up to the house at about a quarter past three that morning. An eerie chill swept over my body as I felt something touch my neck. Weird sounds came from the hedges; I looked and noticed that there was movement. I thought it might have been a racoon or some nocturnal creature. I was right about one thing, it was nocturnal but it wasn't a racoon. Whatever it was had moved along the hedges over to the trees out back. My eyes followed the movement, the savage rustling sounds were too obvious to miss. It seemed like Uncle Earl and Aunt Lucy did not hear or they were so used to hearing these sounds that it never bothered them.

"Uncle Earl, Aunt Lucy? Do you hear these sounds every night, the movement in the bushes?"

"What sounds dearie?" asked Aunt Lucy. She really had not heard a sound. She was loud and tough in arguments but she was a softie and appeared to be afraid of the dark.

"I don't hear anything sonny. I reckon you're tired. Thirteen hours is a really long time to be travelling. You must be bushed! Come on, let's get you inside."

"Yes... I am rather tired. I just need some rest." I know it was not exhaustion, or jetlag or any of that. There was something in the bushes.

"Come on son, I'll carry your bags. Your room is right across the hall from James', we didn't tell him you were coming either. We knew it would turn out to be a pleasant surprise for him."

"Jimmy is here?!" I was excited. Jimmy and I were always close from childhood 'til now, though we hadn't spoken to each other in almost two months. We were almost the same age; he was only a year and four months older than I was. "I can't wait to see him!"

"He's starting university down at U.M. as well, he's taking up some accounting or one of these fancy things that young people go for. I don't know." Uncle Earl said with his usual sarcasm, jerking his shoulders a little. He always was the clown of the family, and knew how to make any situation pleasant.

We got into the house climbing up the stairs leaving the foyer to the first floor. The house was rather large, but very homely. I had been here a few times before, but everything seemed so different. I guess with age I grew an appreciation for the minor details that accompanied everything in life. Getting to my room the first and maybe only thing I saw was the bed. Maybe I was tired after all. I sorted out some of my stuff and took a quick shower before retiring for the night, or what was left of it before the sun rose. I opened the three windows slightly, getting to the third one I felt something. It seemed like something was watching me, studying my every move.

Staring out the window, something came into view. Standing on a branch on a pine tree, I made out a figure watching me intently. I tried to get a better look and noticed immediately that it was not a person and it wasn't an animal either. It looked like a gargoyle but it bore no wings, its ears were short almost like cat ears. Its head was not proportionate according to the rest of its body, a round head that was home to two black shiny beady eyes, eyes that resembled black diamonds with royal blue streaks that sat right above his nose, two small holes placed evenly on an arc shaped projection. The figure was hairless with completely grey velvety skin that appeared rubbery and wet, almost slimy.

An elf stood taller than the creature staring at me, it stood about two and a half feet from its head down. The more I looked, the more I noticed. Its hands reached his knees and its feet faced backward. I noticed it from the book of demons that Father Monroe had been using to help with my ability; it was a demon formed using unborn foetuses or unborn children... children that had only been conceived and lived in the womb no more than six months. It was called a douene, pronounced dwen.

They possessed great abilities and were known for causing confusion in adults if direct contact was made with its eyes for more than three minutes; it would hold one under its spell and plant visions into memory. If ever it got hold of a child, it would put it in the same spell the only difference is it would take the place of the child. The only thing that stood out when this was done was that its feet would be left in place of right and right in place of left. The only way of knowing that this switch had taken place is by seeing its feet, which was hard to do because they kept them covered and were masters of deception.

If at any time they were found out, there were various ways the transformation could be reversed: by visiting someone who practiced the dark arts for a fee, going to a priest who would perform a cleansing, doing it yourself by tying its feet together and removing the shoes and placing them on the corresponding feet but this was tricky because they used their deception to fool adults, the only other way which proved the easiest was by the child deceiving the demon as the demon was susceptible to trickery by a child... being a child itself.

As fascinated as I had become with this new creature, I began to feel quite uncomfortable. It jumped from the tree and run through the backyard toward the house. It moved extremely fast for something that short, movement seemed animated and distorted. I was captivated by what I was seeing. The creature began climbing the house, it was not even gripping or using hands, it looked like a spider. Coming back to my senses I started closing the windows, not a minute to spare. It slammed into the middle window mumbling angrily. For the first time I felt truly afraid.

I went to bed uneasy, knowing that there was something strange outside my window. Almost sixteen years of age and I was still seeing monsters and bogeymen. It seemed the older I got the more bizarre these things became. I remembered as a child they never really did much, but as time went by they became more active and vigorous... it seemed that the more I learned about them from Father Monroe, the bolder they became.

The next morning I woke up to Jimmy's voice calling me. "Deshaun?! I don't believe you're here and you never told me you were coming! You little bugger!" He sounded happy and excited.

I opened my eyes just in time to notice him running right at me. He jumped onto the bed and started shaking me. He started tickling me and giving me playful jabs. It had been such a long time that I forgotten how fun the moments we shared were. I was now wide awake and returned the favour, we started play wrestling and nothing was more fun than hanging out with Jimmy. We both started laughing and hugged each other. Having no siblings Jimmy had been my big brother and I always looked up to him. I was sad for a brief moment... Guilt for not keeping better contact over the few weeks had crept in. I felt a bit weird but I also felt calmed and relaxed.

He was the one who gave me the talk about changes, in my body and in others and also about puberty, the talk about certain feelings, the girl talk, the sex talk and all other talks I needed growing up. All our vacations were spent together having fun, playing, riding our bikes, going on hikes and anything else there was to be done even causing mischief every now and then. We spent the next few days getting ready for school, catching up and hanging out. We had grown closer than ever. Jimmy was the only other person I trusted telling everything, my secrets, my fears, problems and issues, I trusted him enough that I told him about my strange and supernatural experiences.

*   *   *

Monday the twenty third of August came upon us quickly; nevertheless I was ready as ever. The first day of school always made me nervous, but this one turned out to be a breeze. School life had been great, it bore its challenges and ups and downs but I did all I could and even more to ensure I would complete my degree on time. I did better, I managed to complete a year earlier. By the end of 2005 I was done and graduated with honours. I spent the time from then up to August of 2009 working with the Bangor Police Department and also with the Department of Anthropological and Archaeological Studies down at the University of Maine. The opportunity to also be able to teach there was one of my major accomplishments.

The time had come for me to leave this place, Friday the twenty third of August 2009; Maine had been good to me but it was time to return home. Home: the place where my heart was supposed to be; the place where I had spent my first fifteen years of life. I loved it there, quiet, serene, peaceful. Nature was everywhere; you could breathe clean air around every corner. No industrial plants, no sky-rise buildings, it was simple. We had cars and other forms of modern life, but with moderation. My greatest years of life before heading out into the world, off to attain a higher education in a place I'd grown to love were spent home.

Paradise: A Hidden Truth

Six years working on getting my Master's Degree, my life had changed dramatically. I never had the time to be a child, never enjoyed the things that typical teenagers did. These things never captured my interest. The most I was interested in was what was considered to be boring. I loved reading, writing, history and anything to do with nature. Food was one of my secret sins, but I was skinny. Nothing about that changed though. Still five feet, nine inches and weighed one hundred and thirty pounds.

I dabbled in teaching while in high school among other things just to get a feel of what my dreams were like when test in reality. I never knew how passionate I would become about it. Teaching was one of the most rewarding experiences ever. I grew even more of a respect for teachers after that. Seeing what they had to go through first hand, all types of children from the good to the bad and from the intelligent to those who needed a boost. All I could do was my best to ensure I left my mark.

I was in love with planes; in fact my friends said I was married to aviation. I had the greatest collection of model airplanes, over five hundred models stuffed in my attic back in Paradise. It was no surprise I got my pilot's license even though my major was world history and cultures. I also got my Associates Degree in Criminal Justice Technology, Studies and Practices.

Back in Paradise Falls, nothing had changed really. The people were still the same, the faces still recognisable. It was great being with my family again. My mother and father were even more excited that I was back than I was. I had applied for a job at the local police department doing evidence processing. I got acceptance before I got there so that was one job that was secured. After getting there I got a job with the historical studies department down at town hall. The police department and historical department shared town hall along with other government agencies. A convenience for everyone as it was a central location, safe and close to everything.

Returning to Paradise had been great I had spent a whole year there getting used to the place and learning all the ropes. I quickly moved up working hard and proving myself as more than just another face or a new recruit. I spent that year learning all there was to know, the towns people, the laws, my colleagues as well myself. I became a bit more outspoken over the years and I realised that I had come to a point that I would not allow anybody to talk down to me. I was only twenty six years old but I had made my name. 2010 had come around and I had enjoyed all of my twenty six years of living. It was not a sweet life and held its ups and downs, at times more trials than not but that's what moulded me.

I was almost done paying off my student loan and that was one of my biggest worries, apart from my parents. Paradise Falls had become home again. Isla de Tesoro had really improved over the years, the policies and procedures were a lot different. Businesses were more efficient and the government had really made a great turn out. The law sector was also doing better, a lot better than I thought ten years would have done.

Chapter 3

Tragedy

Small towns are very tight knit. People are all fairly acquainted with everyone and then there are always the select few hermits who keep away from the locals... Strange, but everyone has their reason for being the way they are. Some reasons deeper than others. Every city, town, village has its secrets... the smaller the town, the bigger the secrets. Many settlements were built on secrets, some good, some worse than others. What others don't know can't hurt them... Or so you'd like to believe.

The warm air filled the sub-rural village of Paradise Falls. It was a moderately sized community, on the tranquil east coast of Isla de Tesoro, bordered by the Atlantic Ocean. The midsummer's wake had washed over the Caribbean Paradise. The sun steadily rose over the quiet, calm sombre picturesque scenery graced by Mother Nature. The reflection on the ocean created the rippling effect of long slender bars of gold perfectly proportioned.

A miraculous beauty many had been deprived of, but all the inhabitants of this somewhat ancient village were lucky to experience such exquisite and spectacular scenery: rivers, waterfalls, streams, creeks and the ocean. The lush green canopies complimented the wondrous escapade that completed the mind captivating beauty. Just a perfect haven tucked away.

Dewdrops lined the leaves and they looked like crystal-plated emeralds. Stunning! The morning crept slowly, almost stagnant, but it was splendid. The chorus of roosters crowing and other sounds of nature added to the ambience-a tropical bliss. The melodious chirps sounded almost rehearsed. The sequential routine of nature was suddenly disturbed as the rattling sounds of birds evading their campsites filled the air.

The only sounds now were that of sirens and horns blaring. Screams had accompanied them now. It was obvious that something terrible had occurred. The daily tropical ensemble seemed to come to a screeching halt. It wasn't common to hear the sounds of emergency vehicles, especially this early-the break of dawn. It was only 5:45am.

Word of the accident spread like a wild bushfire. In only a matter of minutes, the entire village had some knowledge of what had happened. It was like a grapevine, like CNN news. No one knew for sure what had happened except for what seemed obvious. It appeared that five people were the latest victims of another reckless speeding driver. All sad to say were schoolchildren. Seven year old Chauncé Lennox and seven year old Steven Lennox, two brothers, twins, both of the Paradise Falls R.C. Infant School to the most south easterly quarter of the village; nine year old Junior Adler student of the primary school. Jeynna Seymouré, sixteen-year-old senior of the Paradise Falls Secondary School, days away from graduation, and three-year-old Vianca Bruce of the Paradise

Falls Community Preschool, all three schools just yards away from the scene with the day-care not too far off.

Jeynna was flawless, the remake of a goddess. The valedictorian of her school, she was one of the most prominent that others tried to emulate. She so much resembled the Egyptian Princess Cleopatra. Any hope of her being the top graduate of the "class of 2010" now had been crushed, shattered. Junior represented the athletic face of his school. Two spotlights now dimmed and faded, but the brilliant light they shone would remain engraved in our memories.

Chauncé and Steven were new to the village. Mr. and Mrs. Lennox had just moved back from London with their two youngest children following the death of our wealthiest most esteemed member of society, Madame Lenoiré Bontoft; the mother of Mrs. Marié Lennox. How sad that five seemingly innocent lives had been stolen, robbed. They all dazzled like the uninterrupted midday sun. Five youngsters bound to success, a success that would remain a dream.

The most hurtful loss was that of baby Vianca, only three years old. What had she done to deserve this? This poor young girl and family robbed of a future, of an entire life; enough to ravage, terrorize and devastate anyone. Especially being first time parents, it was their only child. Juan and Maiya Bruce had struggled for eleven long years to conceive a child of their own. For every trial they pledged to adopt. Finally in 2006 their prayers were answered, when doctors informed them that Maiya was with child.

The elation that they felt knowing that after eleven long years of trying, that their dreams of having a child of their own had come true; their prayers answered. What more could they wish for? On August 18, 2007 their bundle of joy was welcomed into the world, and into their family of six other children. Their first adopted child was Christie adopted at the age of four in 1996, in 1998 Jeremy who was six, Winisha at ten in 2000, Samuel and Luke in 2003 twins who were six at the time and Akiro in 2005 who was seven.

What evil being was responsible for this? Though Vianca's skull was cracked open, she still shivered and faint cries were heard until she suffocated to death. How do you approach these unsuspecting parents and tell them that their only biological child had died such a horrific and heart-rending death... It was just dreadful and gut wrenching, after years or trying, and finally you give birth to something so beautiful, so astonishing, a piece of you; after three short years for it to be taken away. What cruel fate, what unimaginable pain, anguish and bewilderment they would be sure to face.

All of this created tension; it was enough for the grieving village people to become furious. They all felt the same, they wanted the head of whoever was responsible, and someone had to pay. Their wish was granted, they were deeply moved to see the head of the driver lay on the hood of his Escalade. Eyes wide-open and dilated, mouth open as if in shock. A solitary hole bore straight through the head. It was obvious that he'd suffered a severe head injury, his expression revealing his feeling during his last moments. A tear slid down his already severed head.

The lifeless body of the charming twenty-year-old Jennifer Tiltson sat limp in the passenger seat. This revelation crushed the entire population even more. She was the perfect beauty and she had just married her lifelong sweetheart, Marcus Tiltson, twenty-two, her first and only love since they were kids. This just pointed that Marcus was the driver. The grief, sorrow and pain just added to the gloom.

Monday the 13th of September 2010 had marked one of the saddest days in the history of Paradise Falls; unfortunate events, untimely deaths, turmoil, families torn apart because of the concealment of the truth. All of the lies and secrets were sure to surface; the secrets that made up what this town was built on would surely lead to its downfall. Secrets held by the villagers like prized possessions and riches that would soon be revealed. It was just a matter of time, for a foundation built of straw can only last as long as a lit match submerged in water.

"I saw it, I saw before it happened. I know what happened. You need to listen to me" rushing up to the police responding to the scene was Crazy Pete, the town's crazy person, "I know what happened!"

"I'm sure you do Crazy Pete, we all know what happened too. It was an accident and many lives were lost." Was the response from Officer Andrew Johnson, almost mocking Pete.

"Why don't you listen to me? Because you think I am crazy? I have no say? I have lost all my human rights and just allowed to live on?" returned Pete, clearly aware of what he was saying.

"Oh no Peter, I am listening... and I hear ya loud and clear. I also know you're not crazy, you just have some mental issues that prevent you from being a normal person." Andrew was having fun teasing Pete, he enjoyed belittling anyone especially people he thought were less than he was.

"Enough of that! You have no right to talk to him like that! He is just as human as you or anyone else here!" I hated seeing people treated unfairly. I didn't know this man but I knew that the treatment was not appropriate.

After the scene was cleared and all the evidence was collected, we reopened the roads for service. The head of investigations had already sent out officers to break the news to the families. This was quickly evolving to a state of emergency incident. Everyone was uneasy and a lot more on guard. Isla de Tesoro was always a safe place, now this had just changed that reputation. It was the greatest tragedy recorded in recent times, nothing of this magnitude had happened in over one hundred years. People died every day, but not like this. This brought truth to the saying 'there's a first time for everything'.

The investigation had begun and I was assigned to the case. It was my first major case since moving back. A few years ago there was another incident that was recorded about a missing child and a wife of a diplomat who was found dead. Some of her parts were missing. Another name linked to the victims was Madame Lenoiré Bontoft; it seemed that her family had been very ill-fated as if her name was cursed and all her family doomed to face short comings.

Chapter 4

Mourning

A pattering rain swept over, side dishing the sorrow and tears. It added emphasis; this hour fresh incident had brought the entire village body to a screeching halt. More and more, the news like an epidemic spread island wide. Never had this happened or anything even remotely close. It reminded me of the past days of war in Russia and Germany. It was proof for the saying, "There's a first time for everything." Yet this was too much to stomach all at once. Emotions run wild; the thoughts that had developed in people's heads were that of insanity. Tears came easy as bloom came to a rose.

Days had passed and the families along with the community board had planned a grand funeral ceremony. It was to celebrate the lives, rather than to mourn the deaths. The wear was strictly 'happy' colours, only radiant coloured clothes were to be worn, as dull colours or colours associated with death would only make the situation more gloomy and sombre. It was one of the worst acts of violence in decades.

All wondered who was responsible for this, and on what grounds. It was destined to scar our people, but we were strong enough in the past, and united we'd make it through this. The investigation had brought no new evidence except for the lone wound inflicted on Marcus Tiltson. It seemed at an instant to be from some high velocity weapon but there was an entry wound with no shell casings or anything else that suggested that gun play was involved. The details of the preliminary investigation were still far too gruesome and unbearable to share with the public. So many lives cut short, so many hearts broken, dreams shattered, families torn apart.

The town came together as any small town would in times of loss. They run fund raisers, held town meetings, and board meetings. They did all they could, being this was the first time we had ever encountered anything as dreadful as this.

There were wakes held by various organisations, donation boxes all over town. Black bows and ribbons dressed buildings over the towns. The churches had draped their pillars and columns with beautiful reefs and purple bows and banners with words of sympathy, condolence and comfort. It was only minutes till our next briefing with various law and government representatives, as well as the professional team working on the incident.

"If we are to have a mass funeral, it must be held at the Catholic Church! It is on hallowed ground and all the lives lost grew up in the Catholic faith. No ifs ands or buts about it! A mass funeral in the open on ground that has not been consecrated will open portals, and that can only lead to demonic invasions, possessions, and who knows what else can happen? We all know that having a history like ours, what doors will be opened. We are still paying for the deals that were made ages ago.

"We still cannot cross The Devil's Bridge from midnight to sunrise; you believe this is a trick of some sort? This bridge was built way before we had the means of constructing a structure of this magnitude. For those of you who do not know what I am speaking about, I will share with you. I did not believe myself, for years I took all these stories as just that- stories. To every story is a degree of truth." pleaded Miss Charlene Rogers, the funeral home director.

"What are you getting at Charlene?!" argued Mr. Anthony Hank.

"Please let's not turn this into another one of those who knows best battles. Miss Rogers, I totally agree and understand. We have lived and sat on our secrets for too long, and we teach each generation that comes along to do the same." added Mrs. Judith Sayers.

"You people and your simpleton ways, your narrow-minded and ancient beliefs; you are all naive with your adolescent fantasies. None of you are anything. All worthless! Every last one of you is pathetic. It's like being in high school all over again. A bunch of small minded people and I am forced to be on a board with you all!" shouted Anthony.

"Mr. Hank, if I may-" Miss Joanne Eugene started.

Cutting her short was another ego trip from Anthony, "If you may what? Say some more dumb nonsense, collaborating with the rest of these fools? After all I expect nothing more from any of you."

"I think you are out of line sir, everyone here has a right to speak and a right to their opinion. Might I remind you this is a board, and not a place to vent issues because we are unsatisfied with our lives and unhappy with ourselves! You always get your chance to speak, with no interruptions from anyone else but the moment someone else has something to say that doesn't fit into your little world you fuss like a menstruating cheerleader." I had to deliver my piece. Every meeting since I got here and was appointed to the board, it had been like this, another of Hank's power trips.

"First off, I am not a sir. I work for a living. Secondly, no little punk fresh out of high school is going to come here and test me!" Hank returned.

"Interesting, so you really think that's what this is about? You think that I am trying you or trying to test you? Honestly, I don't think you'd stand a chance and to rectify the high school situation, that was over ten years ago. You are not of any importance to me and your existence in my opinion is questionable. To cure that wave of ignorance, I am well equipped with my Master's Degree and the experience to go along with it, unlike you. Why is it that your resume boasts you and gives such high favour, but we have never received confirmation of any of your accomplishments?

"I suggest before you tackle me, Shaun Snow, you should know that I do not stand for nonsense from anyone, especially a bigot like you. I will stand up to you, and surely I will be the one to out your fire. You do not own any of us here, you don't own this town, this board, and you definitely have no ownership to me. The days of slavery are long gone, so if that's how you want to live, I suggest a one way trip to the past... and for clarification, no one forced you to be on this board, you applied for the position."

"Look here boy-"

"Hold up! Boy? I am not your boy!" my voice raised I was infuriated. "You believe that because you come from a line of slave drivers that you can just talk to anybody as you please? Let me rectify this with you right now, the colour of my skin does not make me any less than you. I notice the remarks you make and the little statements you cast off to others all the time and this is going to stop! I may be new on this board, and the youngest at that, but I am not dumb. I pay close attention and if there's one thing I do, it's my research. I know all there is to know about you, so I suggest you tread lightly."

The other board members were shocked and appalled; no one had ever stood up to Hank before. They all saw the same things, and complained to each other about it, but no one was brave enough to face him. I had been waiting for my moment to have him cross me so I could shrink him down to size and let him know that he was no better than any of us. He never saw it coming, well not from me at least. He looked at me as a child, a rookie.

"How dare you speak to me like this?"

"If you are at liberty to talk to others as you please, there are no boundaries as to how I will speak to or address you. I was raised and taught to respect everyone and my elders, but I was also taught that respect earns respect. From the first day I met you it has been nothing but insults and you degrading everyone, including me. If you feel that you can disrespect me, I will surely not hold back. It's open season.

"You are lucky that I have respect for the other members of the board, because the things that are on my mind to say to you right now are even a shocker to me. I advise that you take that ego, and take that attitude and have it checked. There are a few places I would tell you to put it but I will not go there. This is not about any of us, or you for that matter. This is about the community and standing together as one, representing our steadfast and unswerving loyalty to each and every member of Paradise Falls."

A silence fell upon the room. It was so quiet that we could hear the swallowing and breathing of everyone in the room. In my mind I was a bit upset that this happened at a meeting to plan the funeral for the victims, but at the same time I felt a euphoria for having stood up to Anthony Hank. Looking around at the faces of the others, they seemed a bit frightened, but they all stayed quiet.

"Ehmm-hmm-ehm", Miss Rogers cleared her throat "right... so... where were we?" She paused for a while looking around as if to make sure everyone was back in their element.

"Yes we were at the point of settling the location for the funeral and since it is a mass funeral and we are left to take charge of the proceedings, we will go ahead and have it done on the church grounds as mentioned earlier." continued Mrs. Sayers.

The meeting went on for over two hours, settling details for the funeral services. A funeral program had been planned and all the costs and fees that were needed had been calculated. We made sure that the families would not have to pay anything out of pocket. The proposal we had arranged was printed and prepared for approval or changes by the families of the victims.

The following day we sat with the families and went over everything. They brought pictures to be included and prayers and poetry and short stories that they wanted included in the funeral program leaflets. It was a very solemn and sad situation to meet to discuss something like this. Emotions were askew, tears, sadness, anger, resentment all fluttered across the room; a room of grieving families and the board members who did not know what to say to sooth the suffering. At times like these, nobody really knows how to begin to console anyone in this situation especially if you have never experienced it yourself.

Anything that was said had to be carefully thought of because the last thing that anyone wanted was to say something that may come off as insensitive or disrespectful, making the families feel like we were downplaying their situation and their anguish. Offering our help and comfort and listening to their stories and their memories of their loved ones who had passed away was the best we could have ushered at that moment. It's a good thing that Anthony had not been present; knowing his reputation had he been there everything would have gone haywire.

All the details were finalised, the date had been decided upon Monday the 27th of September 2010. The day that the deceased would be laid to rest, the first step to closure as the bodies were put to their final resting place. A celebration of the lives and times spent together. Setting free their spirits by slowly letting go of their earthly presence, this would not be easy but it was the beginning to the end and the end of a beginning. An offering of their deliverance and helping their spirits move on to the next life.

With everything going on, I could not rule out the possibility of mystic interference, what if it was a curse used, then that would mean that our department would not be able to solve the case with a standard investigation. There was nothing ordinary about the events surrounding that day. Usually there would be something at the scene, enough to link us to someone but there was none of that and no leads. More and more it started to seem like pure evil was conjured.

The first press release was an absolute mess; Andrew Johnson was assigned to head it as most of us were busy on other detail. He made a complete mockery of the entire ordeal and made the chief who was also absent look incompetent. The entire crew from the department handling the case had to be present for the next briefing and to be prepared for the next meet with the press. Chief Tubbs insisted that if we can't say anything sensible about the case that we lie and make up a story believable enough to distract everybody long enough; lies that could easily be proved or presented as hard evidence. He wanted to make the incident seem like it was a murder and we were doing all possible to find the shooter or suspects involved, though all the evidence proved otherwise. He was sure that because of the wound on Marcus Tiltson we would be using the crime card.

Chapter 5

Revelations

"What the heck is going on in my town people?!" bellowed Chief Tubbs. "I need to know everything. I need reviews of all the evidence, all files! Johnson, what do you have for me?!"

"Well sir this was like something we have never seen. All the evidence and files and all else collected at the scene, says that this was no accident."

"So what are you telling me?!" bellowed Tubbs.

"Well sir, there was no foreign DNA samples collected from the scene, everything found belonged to the victims. Well not the victims but the deceased."

"How can everything at the scene belong to the deceased? Were there no shell casings found? What did you people retrieve?"

"Chief, if I may? The only thing that was found was a gold coin." interjected Lieutenant Amber Griffith.

"A coin? A blasted coin!"

"Yes sir, a coin. I don't know much about it-" said Andrew

"What do I pay you guys for?" interrupted Wiggin. "I have a town full of people here who will not just sit back and relax! They want answers, I want answers! We did terrible at the first press release, we had no formal statement. We looked like a bunch of brain-dead fools! Headless horses being led by blind equestrians through foreign terrain! They want a story and in an hour we better have something to give them!"

"Well sir, we got files back from forensics, and we got a lot back about the coin. This coin is estimated to be about four thousand years old. It was dated to very ancient times, even before the birth and life of Christ.

"Latin inscribed on the coin 'NIHIL SIT SINE EIUS OPPOSITUM', which in English translates to 'Nothing exists without its opposite'. With that said, a further look into the coin revealed some deep dark secrets. This is the foundation on which Paradise was built." Expressed Latricia Moore, head of the Paradise Forensic Anthropology Department at the Paradise Community College.

"Our town of Paradise Falls was once a part of a town named Truth and Consequences. Not much is known about the exact location or whereabouts or what other towns made up this town, but the fact still remains.

"According to legends, which I am not saying is factual in any case but there is enough evidence to support this legend; legend had it that Truth and Consequences was the place where the first settlers inhabited. The first inhabitants were known as Amerindians, from South America divided in to two primary groups or tribes: the Caribs, thought to be of a ferocious warlike nature and the Arawaks, thought of as a peace loving tribe.

"Both groups were said to practice certain methods of worship which included ancient magic, spells as well as curses.

Over the years the Arawaks were said to be chased by the Caribs, chasing them as they went more northerly. The Caribs produced formidable warriors, but with the Arawaks their focus was practicing more of the farming and fishing and building pottery which had been things practiced by both tribes respectively.

"While the Caribs trained warriors, the Arawaks decided to go to the gods for their help. They learned new spells and methods of protection, enchantments and also some which proved to be dangerous curses. With this new found power, they didn't need to be physically adept, so they began training their young the ways of nature worship as they called it, or magic as we call it today. Eventually the Arawaks were equally matched with the Caribs; they were a lot more able to protect themselves from attacks and ambushes.

"They used magic and spells to put enchantments on certain places and used their combined power to build a safety net around their settlements. As they (the Arawaks) got more powerful, the Caribs decided to try new ways of infiltrating Arawak settlements. The Caribs kidnapped members of the Arawaks and forced them to teach them their ways and their enchantments.

"The Caribs used this new learned power to do evil works and started into the way of white magic. White magic was a more advanced form of evil worshiping; it surpassed what we know today as black magic. Most white magic spells and curses required involvement not only with the devil and demons, but it also required raising the dead to do their dirty deeds. The dead bore no souls and no identity, what other way to fool the devil than by his own way? Trickery.

"Eventually the Europeans started invading the small island territories, wiping out most of the Amerindian tribes. They wiped the Arawaks out nearly on the brink of extinction. They didn't do so well with the Caribs, but they ultimately took charge of them, taking over their land and freewill.

"With the remaining Amerindians they used them as slaves, bringing in other slaves from Africa and India and other places where they would hunt for people to work for them and till the soils, work the cane fields and plantations as well as most of the other dangerous jobs.

"All these people came with their own methods of worship. Then voodoo was introduced, as well as black magic and death walkers. Mixing these people created new forms of magic, they all believed in different gods. They started killing the European settlers and revolting. They managed to get their freedom after years of fighting but the Europeans had weapons, while the slaves and others had magic.

"After time passed, the remaining Amerindians, Indians, Africans and others joined forces and escaped to a small section of the island. They used their combined magic and hid their new found settlement, which they called Truth and Consequences. The Europeans were determined to learn of this place and started practicing their own forms of magic, forming cults and other covenants. They learned the deepest darkest magic, tainted with evil. They introduced even deadlier forms of magic and expanded on what the tribes started.

"The Europeans also learned of people who practiced the dark arts from other places in Europe and brought them to populate this island as well as others. They found the town called Truth and Consequences and wiped out most of the people who were left there, but little did they know, these people allowed themselves as sacrifices to protect their town. This was the ultimate sacrifice, for no sacrifice was greater than one's own soul or life to do good for others; it's considered an exceedingly selfless act which is highly regarded. A sacrifice like that is in no comparison to giving up your seat on a flight so another can go in your place; it is way deeper than that.

"With that done, a part of Truth and Consequences had been lost forever, the remaining survivors took refuge and placed more enchantments on the town. Not much is known after that about the unknown part of Truth and Consequences, but many have speculated as to its location.

"Paradise was an old witch coven; the head witch was a woman from the east. She came from Europe when they repopulated the island... No one knew much of her history, where she was from, how old she was, but she was wise, strong and she had a way with words. She always got what she wanted. At the time they didn't know her history or her real name. All they knew is that she called herself Regina Tenebrae.

"Regina Tenebrae sounds like a rather relatively normal name, but some were suspicious of her and thought that there was more meaning to her name. For years they searched for meaning until it was revealed that her true name meant 'Queen of the Darkness' and to those who knew who the queen of the darkness was, knew immediately that she was Lilith. She was the most vile and powerful sorceress who had been stealing souls and living on for centuries maybe even longer.

'Rumour has it that she still lives on today, changing forms and stealing souls as she keeps herself alive. That is according to legend and hieroglyphics left behind by these people."

Her insightful admission had left the room a bit confused. No one knew that part of our history in that way, well at least none of us present. We knew about the changes and the fights and the Amerindians but this was definitely more than we learned in history class. Paradise Falls known slogan was 'Time never stops'. Now laid on the table was ancient history, our old slogan 'Nothing exists without its opposite', had puzzled everyone at the briefing. We really didn't know as much as we thought about our little town.

Latricia had conducted my interview and hired me for the job. When I first returned to Paradise she run me through the ropes and gave me the rundown and provided me the resources I needed. She was a year younger than me, which made it easier for us to work with each other, we understood each other. There was clearly more to this story, more to this history and I had to do my research. I was determined to find out everything there was to know about this dark past and about this case, especially since I had been assigned to it. It was my first case in Paradise Falls and I was determined to do all it took to help solve it.

"So you're suggesting that some kind of voodoo or witchcraft was used to do this whole thing?" asked Chief Tubbs.

"I'm saying keeping an open mind to all the possibilities will leave no sources uncovered therefore giving us a better chance at collecting evidence or substantiation and getting better leads offering us a better likelihood of solving this case. No matter how out of the ordinary or unorthodox this may seem, I have seen cases solved with the introduction of research or insight of people who are known for specialising in that realm of business."

*　　*　　*

"I need to be allowed to make a statement. I saw something. I am still a citizen and I am aware of my rights. Somebody needs to listen to me." Crazy Pete pleaded.

"You want to give a statement?" Andy joked, making a scene and acting like a child.

"Why don't you act your age and do your job?" Pete replied getting frustrated.

"You want to tell me what to do? You crazy fool? Nobody cares what you have to say, no one wants to hear from you. The entire town is waiting for you to die. So why don't you just do us all a favour and get to it?"

Just in time to hear what was going on Amber Griffith walked in. She heard everything from her office. Enraged and furious, she rushed towards the front desk where Andrew had been harassing and disrespecting Pete. Amber was locked and loaded; she'd had enough of the way people who were supposed to be the professionals were acting especially towards the locals. Storming towards him, he managed to look up and spotted her coming. It was too late for him.

"Is this the way you behave on a regular? Have you no decorum, no behaviour? You want to treat everyone like a child, and you act high and mighty just because you wear a police uniform? Might I remind you that you only wear this uniform because your father served this island and did a damn good job at it! He respected everyone and treated everybody with dignity! You are thirty six years old, is that really your level of maturity? You never qualified for this job and had I any say in the matter you'd have never ever even been considered to become a janitor for this office! Do you still want to taunt this man and treat him like he is nothing, because there is a lot more where this came from and I bet you don't want me to go any further? I assure you that you will not like the outcome!" Amber had unloaded a bomb on Andrew.

He stood there dumbfounded, his face turned red. The embarrassment he felt could have been seen from all corners. It was obvious that no one had ever said anything to Andrew about his behaviour prior to this but it was about time someone did. Everyone stood around just looking in amazement. Nobody knew what to do, if they should cheer or applaud, they were even afraid to smile or laugh so they all stood quiet.

"What are the rest of you looking at? You all have jobs to do. This is not the circus!" She spoke sternly, looking around at the crowd that had formed.

Crazy Pete stood there unmoved, he had a slight smile on his face, "Thank you Lieutenant, I've been trying since the accident to be heard and nobody will hear me out."

"I apologise for that Mr. Peter Thomas, and I also apologise for that behaviour. If you would, please follow me to my office, I'll take your statement there."

"Thank you very much, I appreciate that and it's no problem you have nothing to apologise to me for. I would have done the same, but they'd maybe just throw me in jail."

She laughed, blushing. Trying to hide it she looked away. She walked him over to her office and allowed him to have a sit. Walked over to her desk and found her pen and witness statement forms and the other documents required to begin her interview. She sat down and started writing her information down on the paper, date and time. She prepared her stamps to officiate the documents and left everything sitting for when she was ready. It was customary for her to use a tape recorder for every interview she conducted.

Over the intercom, "Shaun Snow, this is Lieutenant Amber Griffith, could you please come to my office. We have a witness here who'd like to give a statement for the recent incident and I'd like for you to sit in for this."

"No problem Lieutenant, I'll be right over." This was my first time being put on a case since I joined the Paradise Falls Police Department. To me it was an honour, a case of this magnitude and I was considered to assist. I hurried over to her office, tape recorder in my top pocket already turned on so I could record everything for my personal files to review.

I got to her office and sat down next to the witness. I had noticed him from around town, but I never knew who he was. He had always just sat about on a porch, Twenty Lime Stone Road. He just sat there, it didn't seem like he had friends or family and if he did they had for some reason all abandoned him. Still a bit nervous and anxious, I introduced myself and prepared for the interview.

"Sir, do I have your permission to record and document this interview?"

"Yes Lieutenant Griffith, you do."

As things proceeded she wrote as it went along. "Can you please state your name for the record?"

"Peter Alexandre Thomas, with an R.E."

"Thank you for that." She said with a warm smile. "Can you please tell me to the best of your ability what you remembered and if you could the dates or possible times of the incidents?"

"Yes Lieutenant Griffith that will not be a problem."

"You may begin at any time Mr. Thomas."

"Well on August eighth, I went up to the countryside over in Rouge Hill to tend to my farm and garden. I must have lost track of time because when I looked up the sun began setting so I knew it was time to wrap up and head back to town. I usually take a bath in the river each afternoon before I head back to town, and I figured not because it was nearing dark and nightfall would be soon didn't mean I couldn't still take my bath.

"So, I packed my stuff and placed them in my shed and walked down to the river naked as I always would, with my bucket in hand so I could carry some water back to the shed after my bath to pour over me to get rid of any dirt or anything I picked up on my way back to the shed. On my way down there, I heard voices, like two people having a conversation. So I walked slowly, careful not to make any noise. I wondered who was on my property; I thought maybe there... maybe it was the thieves who had been stealing my crops. So I picked up a stick not thinking much of it.

"I continued walking toward the voices, careful not to make any sounds or even to be heard, it was awfully dark but I managed well. As I got closer I noticed a glow like a bright light and from a distance it seemed like a torch. You know like one of them tiki torches? So I just continued carefully toward it. As I got closer, I noticed it wasn't at all a tiki torch..."

He paused, he seemed frightened and his eyes had gone watery. Lieutenant Griffith offered him some tissue and placed the box on the desk in case he needed to reach them at any time. She seemed a bit confused; she looked scared as well just looking at his expression. I began to feel cold chills. This was weird, nothing has happened yet I told myself.

"Mr. Thomas? Are you okay?" she asked calmly.

"Yes Lieutenant Griffith, I'm fine. I know everyone thinks I am crazy and this might not help one bit with that, but I know what I saw and I know this is important to solving this case and many others."

"Don't you worry Mr. Thomas; if you need to take a break that's okay and we can continue as soon as you are prepared."

"That's alright, I'll continue."

"Thank you."

"Yeah, so I got closer and closer and as I saw it wasn't a tiki torch... in fact it wasn't any torch. It was just a huge ball of fire It was much bigger than a car tire. I couldn't quite see clearly so I continued going towards the river bank. As I got closer I noticed the fire was on the other side just a little lower down from where I stood.

"What's funny is that fire... there was no wood or anything. It was just a huge flame, a raging ball of fire, and it wasn't on the ground like a bonfire or anything. It was suspended in the air almost but not quite. It was half in the water and half out. I thought that there was maybe a tree or something that someone set fire to, but it wasn't because I went a bit closer to get a better look, still trying not to get too close to be seen or heard.

"I was finally close enough to see and hear everything and I overheard a conversation... at first I thought that there were maybe fifteen people or more, but it was only one person and that fire. I never expected what I saw really. I thought for a moment that I might be going crazy. The person with that fire and talking to it, having a conversation. First off a fire then this person..."

"You saw a fire and a person and heard many voices maybe more than fifteen?" Amber asked clearly confused and puzzled, it didn't seem like she was buying his story, on the other hand I listened attentively, paying special attention to his story and his demeanour. I thought that he was telling the truth, he seemed scared as he got to that part.

"Yes maam', I kid you not. I swear to God and on all my earthly possessions I saw a fire and a lady and heard voices."

"Okay Mr. Thomas, please continue." She ushered.

"So there is this fire and... and..." He paused again tears in his eyes. He seemed even more terrified, it was as if he was reliving the moment and it was on replay in his head.

"Mr. Peter Thomas, sir, please there is no need to be scared or to feel any way. If you need some time or anything perhaps a drink, maybe coffee, tea or water I'd be glad to get it for you." I offered.

"I know but see, when people think you are crazy and you see something like this... it kinda makes it hard to tell others and have them believe you. I already have no credibility and a permanent label... I'm sorry, I will continue... May I have some coffee please?"

"I'll get that for you Mr. Thomas" Offered Amber getting to her percolator and preparing it to begin a fresh brew of coffee.

"Thank you Lieutenant Griffith." he answered. He seemed quite pleasant and respectful.

He continued his recalling of the encounter. "The fire, there was someone with the fire. She kept referring to the fire as master. I heard the fire speak and the voices, all the voices it seemed like so many of them. Every time the fire spoke, it was these voices. A talking fire and Madame Lenoiré Bontoft. I know what you're thinking, fires don't talk and Madame Lenoiré Bontoft has been dead for some time... I know this well because I work at the cemetery; my house is on the cemetery land as the crypt keeper. I dig the graves and almost all the maintenance down there, I dug her grave myself and I buried her too.

"But there she was, alive as you or me or any live person with this fire. This fire with so many voices, it seemed like more than a fire. I thought it was some special theatrical performance like a Hollywood movie or something with all the fancy special effects, but this is Paradise Falls, we don't have any of that stuff out here. I listened to what was being said and what I heard freaked me out even more. I mean a dead lady and a fire... talking."

"Mr. Thomas, what are you saying? The fire was talking and there was a dead woman talking as well? Sir, I find this all a bit hard to believe." questioned Amber.

"Yes a talking fire and Madame Lenoiré Bontoft were having a conversation. I find it just as hard to believe as you Lieutenant, but I know what I saw and I also know what I heard."

"Maybe we should allow Mr. Thomas to continue his account of the events of that night." I interjected.

I wanted to know more. As much as the story seemed a bit farfetched, I had seen things myself and heard things so I knew there was a great possibility that he was telling the truth. Unless this was some elaborate hoax, but why would he go through all that? It made no sense. There was no reason to lie or make up such a tale so he had to be telling the truth. He already had the name Crazy Pete around town. I doubt he would do anything to make it worse upon himself. My curiosity had peaked and his story was too strange to be made up.

"Thank you Mr. Snow. I know this all sounds crazy but I am not lying."

"Do not worry Mr. Thomas; we are not here to judge you. Please continue with your statement." I added.

"So the fire and Madame Lenoiré Bontoft were deep into this conversation, at first she looked like herself. She appeared regular then she slowly transformed... she changed, she didn't quite look like herself anymore. She was a lot different like an animal, and her skin was scaly... she looked like a lizard or a frog or a dragon; I know it was her. She was naked in the water facing the fire as they spoke. Her eyes were glassy and a blackish green type colour.

"I overheard her telling calling the fire 'master'. The more the fire spoke the more voices I heard. It was like an army in perfect unison or a choir in harmony. I don't want to beat around the bush but she was making a deal with this demon thing... a deal with the devil. It said to her about she had been losing her touch and she needed to make sacrifices to keep living. He called her Lilith a few times when he spoke of her accomplishments and the things she had done to make him proud.

"He told her that she needed to do something big in order to keep her title and her position, because there was new blood in line for her position and she needed to defend it. He told her what to do and how to do it. She had to kill Marcus Tiltson the morning of the accident before he left his home and Anthony Hank would use the demon used for the death curse and command it into his lifeless body.

"The demon would lead his wife Jennifer to ride with it and Hank would conjure the spell to kill Jennifer and her unborn child. Another demon had been placed into her weeks before to torment her and by the day of the accident it would take control of her so she would not be able to take the wheel after Anthony had instructed the demon to careen off the road into Jeynna Seymouré, Junior Adler and Vianca Bruce.

"The entire accident was planned to- to kill her daughter's twins and that unborn baby, and Vianca Bruce. The twins were my nephews, Chauncé and Steven. Madame Lenoiré is a witch! She is evil. She killed my wife and took my daughter. She is not dead.

"She changes bodies every few years and takes over the life of some innocent woman with a family. Her real name is Lilith... I-I... I have evidence to prove my story. I would never make this up. Anthony Hank is her slave; he sold his soul to her years ago. He has no credentials but landed all these jobs and positions. No one can find anything to corroborate his accounts of his past, but even if all of that is obvious... he is still feared, he can't be fired.

"It's like he has power over others, but only certain people are immune to this... people like you Shaun. You are the one they fear most. I heard the demon telling her about you and how they need to eliminate the threat and you're being protected by the Light. You are a pharus, but you were born a pharus so that makes you a lux.

"I looked into it and found a great deal of information. They cannot harm you, though they try. You see weird things don't you?"

Chapter 6

Unlucky Sevens

All that Mr. Thomas said was crazy; it was so crazy there was no way he made it up, he almost sounded like a fanatic. It was one of these situations where the crazier the tale got, the more authentic it became. Knowing about the things I had seen over the past few years and some of the stories Father Monroe had told me, Peter's story started to make even more sense, it became a reality. It was logical, and the account was too precise. I even had images as he told the story. The details were too precise, and why would he want to make up something so bizarre, so out of the ordinary, he was already known around town as Crazy Pete. There is no logical reason why he'd provoke it any further. He didn't strike as the attention seeking type. I didn't know much about him until now, but what I saw of him in the few moments gave a lot more than what was needed. I was not eager to judge, but I had put my conviction and faith not only in what he said but also in him.

Furthermore, he spoke about his dead wife and his daughter who went missing and were never found. He broke into tears, his voice, his body language; his whole behaviour suggested he was being sincere. I know for sure he was not making any of that up. No one would create a tale so farfetched about their loved ones, especially if they loved them and they had died. It made no sense.

The more I thought about it, the more I needed to know. I listened to the tape I recorded during his witness statement over on continuous replay. His admission served a great deal, the information he gave was a lot more than we had. We didn't even have any leads but now we had enough to work on. Though it was not professionally sound or admissible in court, it was all we had to work with. In all honesty, Peter's narrative sounded more commonsensical.

According to the department, we did not even have a crime so we were basically investigating evidence and hoping for the best. There was no murder weapon, no weapon at all, no foreign finger prints. Murder was ruled out completely. Marcus Tiltson didn't appear drugged or under the influence of any strange matter or substances. Tests run at the scene corroborated that. Eyewitness' admissions gave nothing more than the obvious; nothing more than what was identifiable to the naked eye. The only thing that really stood out was the silver coin.

Things kept on replay in my head. Wonder, questions, everything about that horrible day seemed wrong, just how it happened. All of a sudden it didn't seem like an accident, nor did it seem like it was intentional on Marcus's part. Something was just not right. The twins, her own grandchildren and she had them brutally murdered; she killed them herself but how? She was not at the scene, she could not have been at the scene, and she was dead. She set up this whole elaborate accident to take seven lives, seven innocent lives. Jeynna Seymouré, Junior Adler, Chauncé and Steven Lennox, Vianca Bruce, Jennifer and Marcus Tiltson, seven lives that were no more; how did she do that from six feet under?

Strange how something that takes years to create can be destroyed in the blink of an eye. Here today and gone tomorrow, that's the reality of life that most never really accept.

     The autopsy results were finally in. I went over them carefully, the gruesome and gory details started to haunt me. I remembered the day of the accident, all the chaos, lifeless bodies all mangled up, blood and body parts and the smashed vehicle. The faint cries of a suffering Vianca echoed, slowly suffocating to death while choking on her own blood. The severed head of Marcus Tiltson and the solitary tear that slowly slid down his face as his eyes and mouth stood wide open as he lay in deathly surprise.

     As I began reading the contents of the coroner's reports and the notes to go along, I felt uneasy; a build-up in my chest almost like my breathing was being constricted. There were not seven coroner's reports as I expected, there were eight. The eighth had no name, it only said 'unnamed unborn child'. There was no way that Peter could have known according to the report Jennifer the infant's deceased mother herself didn't know that she was pregnant. There were no indications of a pregnancy either. None of her family or friends mentioned her being pregnant. The couple desperately wanted a child; they thought it would complete their dreams and they would have finally begun the family that they always hoped for. I had to find out more about them, more about Pete. He knew something no one else knew, not even our detectives; something that was only discovered after the autopsy was completed.

On Marcus's report it spoke of an entry wound to the forehead and also of his severed head. The wound responsible for his death was whatever had decapitated him. The report also stated that the wounds inflicted had no residue, no samples of any metal or alloy or anything else. The causes of the wounds were deemed as unknown. The more I read the more I became interested in speaking to Peter, the only source that started to make practical sense.

For the other victims, the reports confirmed that the accident was not the cause of death; an impact so physically powerful, but still not the cause of their deaths. What killed these people? The report of baby Vianca also made no sense, her wounds were not caused by the impact or the fall, her skull split open before the impact. The only death that made sense was that of the unborn baby. Most of the reports stated undetectable causes, and all the causes of death were deemed unnatural.

I went over to Latricia Moore's office; I needed her to hear the tape of the interview, and to deliver to her the written witness statement Amber had recorded. As I got there she was reviewing the autopsy files. The look on her face was so intense as she read her eyes concentrated on the details of the reports. So many pages to go through that said nothing. Her hand covered her mouth as she turned the page, she started crying. I couldn't stand it; I went over to her and tried to console her. As I looked I noticed she was on the files for the unborn baby. After getting back a moderately normal state, we compared notes and our thoughts on the autopsies.

"Shaun I know many people are not keen to or open to things that they don't understand, and fear of the unknown leads people to do and say crazy things. Ever since I moved here to Tesoro, I've been reading into the history and doing research and interviewing some of the older residents and slave descendants. The things I learned at first were a bit odd, just unusual stories, but not all that unusual. The stories were just different, of a different nature. I must admit that I've heard similar stories before, but I never expected to be living one. I mean the thrill of hearing a horror story; a good horror story is always solicited. I'm sure I'm not the only one who delights in such, even a guilty pleasure of all of us deep within is seeing or experiencing, but the truth is many of us are not prepared for the truth."

She had a point, many people always ask for the truth and honesty but when it is presented to them they get emotional and go to extremes and take things overboard. The easiest thing to tell is the truth, because there is not much work or effort needed, while with a lie it requires so much more work. With a lie you need an impeccable memory, and one lie is never ever sufficient because in order for the first lie to be fool proof you needed a series of lies. The prerequisites to be a liar, the obligations asked for in order to be a great liar were far too extensive, and all lies eventually come to light.

"I identify with that in its entirety, I've heard some legends and as a child I even saw things I didn't understand and according to others it was just my imagination... at times I believe my imagination might have followed me past teenage years and even into adulthood." I joked with the truth not giving off too much. It felt like I was lying.

She chuckled and laughed, blushing a little she finally said, "You are too much."

"Why thank you, I take that as a compliment. All jokes aside though I do see strange things, but they're not so strange when you think about it. If you believe in angels and saints and all these things, then there is the opposite to consider as there are fiends, demons, devils and sprites and other evil spirits. The old town slogan is nothing exists without its opposite, and that is to me something that goes without saying. To light there's darkness, to good there's bad, and all these others."

She seemed to be in deep contemplation, meditating on the words I had just spoken. She didn't look surprised or shocked; it seemed to all sink in with reasoning. I wondered what was on her mind. It seemed like time had stopped while I wait but time never stops, never slows down, time is always constant. She fiddled with her fingers like she wanted to say something but didn't know how.

Then she blurted out, "Shaun, do you believe in curses and voodoo dolls?"

"Well yes, I do."

"At the scene of the incident, there was no weapon and injuries inflicted but no evidence of the injuries happening to the victims physically. It's as if they were harmed from another place. Reading the autopsy and reviewing all the remarks and the organ sheet and everything else, my thoughts were all over and the more I thought, the more likely the answer to my question pointed more towards voodoo dolls."

I didn't think of that possibility. It never even crossed my mind, something so simple since the wounds were not directly

inflicted it could have been a curse or voodoo dolls or anything
that used evil. The thoughts started pouring in and even Peter's
story about the devil and the dead woman tied nicely into this
theory. It seemed to an extent as the only possible explanation.
How else could this have happened? There were no foreign prints,
residue, nothing that should have not been there and nothing that
should have been either. The confusion made perfect sense, it's
like the mystery was solved but still we needed to prove this. We
needed to get whoever was involved, whoever was responsible had
to be found.

"Voodoo dolls...Voodoo dolls?" I repeated aloud not
conscious of saying anything. My mind was working overtime, I
was in the realm. "It makes sense."

"Yes, voodoo dolls. I researched it and I found out some
extensive information."

"It makes perfect sense. I have something I need you to
read and a tape here to listen to." As I spoke I handed her a copy of
the tape and Mr. Thomas's witness statement.

She took the file and played the tape as she read. With
every word that replayed, every gripping detail, every piece of his
account her expression changed. It was as if she had heard of
similar accounts or maybe read about it before. She never expected
it to become part of her reality. Tears welled up in her eyes, tears
of terror. The fright was visible, her skin rippled with goose
bumps, she was having chills. The more that was revealed on the
tape, she seemed to grow more terrified, more hesitant. She closed
her eyes as Peter's voice spoke of the slaying of the victims.
Horror in her eyes, questions. Then it came to the real surprise, she

never expected it. She gasped, and started crying unstoppably as Peter spoke of the unborn child.

I sat back as I listened in, though I had heard the tape countless times already during the course of the day it was like I was hearing it for the first time. Some things I had missed or neglected or over looked, things that I had passed on as irrelevant started to come together. Every word, every gripping detail, everything was a crucial point. We had to give Mr. Thomas a visit. He was the only one who had stepped forward with anything. What he gave though to others would not seem like much, but it was our entire case and not only confined to Paradise Falls. If this Lilith woman had been living through others for centuries the amount of lives she could have ruined and used as her power cells could be overwhelming, almost insurmountable. This lady left a path of destruction in her wake, and everything she touched was for her own personal gain.

After the tape stopped, she looked at me with a blank expression. As if lost for words, she just sat silent. It was her first time hearing the tape and reading the statement, the pressure that was put on her had her at a loss for words. She just sat speechless her eyes fixed on the statement in her hand. She looked hopelessly at it; it was like she had been beaten to immobility and lay staring at an orphaned child being dragged away by human traffickers as she lay helpless, battered and bruised in her own blood. Dazed and confused, she sat almost comatose not even her breathing was detectable.

Slowly she gained composure. She had been slapped back to consciousness by the invisible hand of reality; she shrugged standing up and looking around the room pacing up and down. I could tell that her thoughts were racing. I was invisible to her for a moment as she tried to comprehend what had just taken place. She paused like she had an epiphany, that eureka moment, the 'ah-ha' complex. Her face lit up, I could almost see the light bulb shining brightly over her head. The smile on her face was almost like an evil grin, she was thinking of something.

"Shaun" she paused for a moment then continued, "why don't we pay Mr. Peter a visit? I'm sure that he'd give us even more of an account off the records. I know this sounds a bit wild, but why don't we give it a shot."

"I was hoping you'd say that."

I felt relieved that she suggested it, that she was the one to say it rather than me. Us having to go over to Peter Thomas's residence needed to be secretive and confidential. The department could not know, due to the circumstances. We needed to find a way to head out to him without rising any alarms or suspicions and we had to make sure that no one caught air of our intentions. We decided that the best way was after working hours around the evening time. We planned to meet up in a discreet location and leave no traceable path that could be easily followed, even though nobody in the department was interested. We also had to worry about what the public might have thought. I wrote a short note to Peter letting him know that Latricia Moore and I wanted to meet him at the most convene place, the church. Nobody would suspect that it was a planned meeting and it was not really a crowded place, especially now that most of the town's people were in mourning and at wakes for the deceased.

On the note I only put specifics, gave him a brief rundown: *'Dear Mr. Peter Thomas, I hope that this will reach you in good light. During your confession I really got answers to a lot of questions that plagued me. I know this is might be asking for a lot, but my colleague Latricia Moore and I would like to have a meet with you down at the Catholic church tonight and discuss some things. I assure you that this will be confidential and you can freely speak about any and everything. Latricia has a bit of knowledge on these things and she has some useful information of her own. This would mean a lot to us and would do a great deal in helping us get closer to understanding everything that has been going on in Paradise lately. Any more information would really help a lot; I know that you have a lot more that you held back. I also have a few questions regarding our meet at the station the other day. This is outside of department proceedings and anything discussed shall remain off the records. Please consider this and feel free to contact me at 712-7849. You may contact me at any time. Sincerely Shaun Snow.'*

I had written the note not knowing exactly what to say. I had met him only once and was not sure of the right approach.

After work I drove down towards the docks, past the fishing depot to the cemetery house where Peter had been staying. The cemetery sat about twenty feet away from the ocean, a small dirt road surrounded by a thick covering of trees drove right between the Catholic half of the cemetery closer to the land, while the other denominational cemetery closer to the seaside. A little distance past the cemetery going up to the Clifton Hill, the road ended and there stood the cemetery house, all by itself. Beyond the house was a vast swathe of foliage, hiding the Ridge Cliffs, a steep precipice type ledge dropping two hundred feet down where the ocean waves pounded violently unto jagged rocks below that created the jaw like surface. The rocks resembled stalagmites, and were jagged and uneven protruding sharply from the ground and ocean floor below. I walked up to the front door, and knocked. I heard shuffling then he came and answered the door.

"Mr. Snow, what a pleasant surprise", he said with an earnest smile on his face, "I didn't expect anyone to take me seriously but I hoped that you would."

"Thank you for receiving me so warmly. I believed everything that you said and I'd really like to speak with you privately. Please have a look at this" I said handing over the note, "feel free to contact me and let me know what you decide, and if you have any suggestions, I'd appreciate that... and please, call me Shaun."

"No problem Mr. Shaun, I am grateful for you stopping by don't get many visitors since I lost my family and the town labelled me as crazy. I'll speak to you tonight. Take care, and drive safely." He turned his back; his cheerful mood had changed, he seemed sad.

He mentioned losing his family. There was a lot more to this man than he let out. He was suffering and deep inside he was still dealing with the loss of his family. I didn't even know he had a family. I somehow felt responsible for finding out more about him, I didn't want to intrude on his personal life or just disregard his rights to his privacy so I decided to wait until night came and we sat with him. Hopefully he would give more; he would open up more, not only about the case, but also about himself, his family and his past. In the words of Oscar Wilde 'Every saint has a past, and every sinner has a future'; for not every slate is wiped clean because of change or secret sins and faults nor is a man's pate cleansed because he conceals his past.

Chapter 7

Secret Gathering

My Phone rang two minutes as I drove back home. I didn't recognise the number, I answered the call and it was Peter, confirming our meet at the church. We decided on six that evening, just about two hours later. Enthusiastic that he had called, I immediately called Latricia and let her know of the development. She was even more thrilled than I was and said she'd be there by quarter to the hour with coffee and cheese croissants. I continued on my way home, taking a quick shower and grabbing a quick bite to eat. As I hung about my room getting ready to head down to the church, I thought about holding my video camera. Capturing the audio would be great, but getting everything on video would make it complete.

I grabbed all I could, and went down to the church a bit earlier. On my way there as I drove past the presbytery, Father Monroe crossed my mind. I thought it a great idea to speak with him and keep him up to speed with the new developments. I went in and there he was in his office preparing for the upcoming funeral. In front of him sat eight folders with the names of the deceased, and the unborn baby. That would make what I was about to tell him a lot less difficult, seeing he had received updates on the victims and the coroner's report, and he also knew about the

Tiltsons' unborn baby. He seemed deeply focused as he flipped through the pages. He hadn't seemed to notice me standing there at the doorway. I knocked on the wooden partition, signalling that I was there. He didn't hear the first time; he was so deep in the zone. I walked a bit closer to the doorway, making gestures with my left hand as I knocked with my right. He still hadn't noticed my presence.

"Good afternoon Father Monroe." I greeted as I knocked even louder, I felt the partition shake. "Sorry for the intrusion, I hope I am not disturbing. I should have maybe called first but I was already on my way to the church and I decided to just drop in seeing the time constraints. Something just came up and at the last minute confirmation was made and I kind of thought of you being part of it."

"Oh... good afternoon there Shaun!" He said raising his head as he watched me for the first time. He really hadn't noticed me. "I'm sorry I did not even notice I had company. That's no problem; I'm not busy at all. Come on in. Just reviewing some files and planning the mass for the funeral. How are you?"

"I'm doing good Father, how about you? How are you keeping up?"

"I'm not bad at all."

"I'm glad that you are. How have the funeral arrangements been coming along?"

"It's been very busy the past couple of days and a lot of controversy surrounding this funeral. Anthony Hank has been trying to protest the funeral taking place at the Catholic Church. It's beyond me why it matters to him that much. He never cared when they were alive, he cared less when the accident happened, so it just makes no sense... that little cretin. I never fancied him much, now I'm starting to dislike certain aspects of him."

It was an unexpected yet pleasant surprise hearing Father Monroe speak that way. When it came to serene, he was the man, he seemed like the master of divinity but Anthony Hank had managed to upset him enough to make him feel ill toward him. It was not hard to believe, Anthony was annoying enough to cause an angel to give up its wings. I had only just met the man and I was so turned off and disgusted by him and his ways, it was so much more than that. I had a boiling anger and rage toward that man. Nobody cared for him much, his smugness, arrogance, conceit, haughtiness the shallow pride, his self-importance and that obnoxious superiority complex; to me he was just an egotistical self-centred prick who still believed he was that popular kid in school and with the impression that everybody wanted to be him or be in his circle. Thankfully, I thought of myself as a square in that equation. I did not like the best bone in Hank's body if he possessed that much.

"I deeply sympathise with you Father... He is quite..." I paused for a while trying to think of a word I could use to describe Hank without disrespecting the priest or the church property, "quite the character that Hank. I've had my experiences with him and there is no reasoning with him. So I can touch the surface of how you feel."

Father Monroe laughed, "Well, that's a lot better put than what I had in mind. I am still human regardless of being a priest."

"Thank God then, I thought I was going a bit far when I thought of him as a person I had grown to detest."

"Well, such is life my child. So as you were saying, what's this about a meeting this evening?"

"Oh yes I'm supposed to be meeting up with Miss Latricia Moore and Mr. Peter Thomas at six over at the church. I'm not exactly an expert at this kind of thing... you know... this supernatural stuff, and Mr. Thomas came down to City Hall and gave a confession of something he saw before the accident. As farfetched as it sounded, I believed him. He even spoke about Marcus and Jennifer's baby, the unborn child. They didn't even know about it. No one really did until the autopsy."

"Interesting... and do you know about Peter's reputation around town, around Tesoro?"

"Yes Father, I do", I felt like he was sceptical, "I know all about him being 'Crazy Pete'."

"And you still believed him..?" It was more of a statement than a question.

"Yes, I believed every word and I believe there is a lot more that he knows that he held back because of the circumstances surrounding him and as well as it being an official admission."

"I am proud of you Shaun. Ever since Pete's unfortunate incident, his misfortune, the town's people have seemed to all shun him. They've all forgotten who he was, who he still is. It seems like a part of history had disappeared, and a new one was created."

"Proud of me?" I questioned as I wondered what I had done. "Proud of me why father?"

"You see Shaun, many things happen, a lot of times things that are questioned with no simple answers, at times even no soluble answer at all. Strange things happen all the time, things that go beyond human comprehension and beyond science, that get labelled as nonsense, or impossible, at times they're completely forgotten. Peter Thomas has been through a lot, I don't know how but he managed to remember a lot of what the others forgot. He still remembers his family, and some other things are sketchy to him, but I cannot just come out and tell him.

"He was cursed and the wrong interference can have catastrophic repercussions. Simply put, if he doesn't remember himself, who he was and all that happened, he will remain this way... suspended in limbo. If anyone who remembers tries to reveal to him the truth, he will go crazy and his life would be meaningless. The thing that saved him from the full effects of this curse was the love he had for his family, and for the people he served.

"Whoever it was who cursed him hadn't bargained for this, they never thought about love. Love is something that curses cannot work on. They never counted on that love being a factor, but it is what saved him, and if I could I would reveal that too, but I'd only cause him more harm. All I can do is sit powerlessly and watch and hope that he remember as the time flies. He still believes that his daughter is alive, and she is."

I stood in shock, absorbing all that Father Monroe had just said... So many things were on my mind, so many questions. My thoughts raced. His sincerity was obvious, he wanted to help but he couldn't. A curse? Peter Thomas was cursed, his wife was killed and his daughter was taken but he remembered that much, and in his heart he knew that she was alive. Maybe that twinkle in his eye when he spoke, that passion, that's what it was. He remembered his nephews, the twins, his sister-in-law's children. I had to help but what could I do? I didn't know much about any of this and I was still trying to get a better understanding of my own situation.

"A curse?" I spoke my thoughts aloud, "Love?"

"Yes Shaun and it's almost six we should head over to the church."

"Right, we should." I said in agreement.

I was still processing everything, that I had almost lost track of time. I was almost in a state of paralysis. This man had been through so much, and was still having to suffer at the hands of others. Dealing with the loss of his wife every day and the disappearance of his daughter- his flesh and blood and having to deal with the dirty snide remarks and name calling from the island people; having to live his life with a tarnished reputation. My heart was overwhelmed, I almost felt his pain. I did not know much about him, but finding this out made me even more empathetic towards him. I gained a new respect for the man behind that solid exterior. Having built a life, a family and to lose it all after working so hard, it just proved that life was a funny thing and reality just the same. You could spend minutes, hours, days, months and years building something and it could all be gone in a matter of seconds. All your hard work and effort turned to nothing, rendered useless. Time had no regard for anyone or anything but time itself.

We headed over to the church, a five minute walk from the presbytery. Latricia was just pulling into the parking lot. We went in and sat down and waited for her to come in. As we waited my mind went astray. Madame Lenoiré had been dead for almost a year now, but she was seen and heard by Peter. She had her grandchildren killed. It was not her, it was a Lilith. Who was this Lilith? The confusion, everything was so complicated. The twins were gone, Peter's daughter was never found. As I thought about everything, Latricia had sneaked up behind me.

"Hey!" she shouted in a whisper, trying not to startle me. "I brought the coffee and snacks." She had a cheerful disposition, she seemed very excited. She looked and noticed Father Monroe. "Oh, I'm sorry Father Monroe, I didn't even realise it was you. I didn't notice it was you without your cassock on."

"It's quite okay my dear, no harm done."

"I hope you don't mind, I'm here to meet with Shaun and Mr. Thomas."

"I don't mind at all." He responded delightfully.

"Um, Latricia, I actually paid Father Monroe a visit before coming here and asked him to join us, I should have said something but it was really last minute." I interrupted.

"I hope that you don't mind my dear child."

Her face lit up like a child at a carnival, "Oh my gosh! I don't mind in the least!" She was blushing, "This is even better than I expected. I didn't bargain for this! Thank you for joining us Father! This is like some super top secret mission and we are a secret society here to solve mysteries and fight crime and such."

I think she was getting carried away, maybe the thrill of doing something different, something new and exciting. We had no orders to do this and no permission. It was like a rogue mission, without the approval of the department, no permit, the thrill of the moment, the adrenaline rush and it was a great feeling. Everything was outside of protocol. She took that rather well. I hoped that Peter would not feel uncomfortable. Just as I thought of him, he walked in. We were all there quite before six, they were awesome time keeps.

"Miss Moore, Mr. Shaun, Father Monroe, a pleasant good evening to all! Glad to be here with you." Peter greeted as he joined us.

"Well, let's get started! I brought refreshments. Feel free to dig in." Latricia said excitedly.

"Okay we all know the basis of us meeting, so there is no need for formalities. I hope we're all comfortable enough." I said almost afraid. I took out the equipment I brought and placed the video camera on the tripod to record as we went along, I also had my tape recorder which I held in my hand.

"I am ready," Peter's voice spoke out. "I need all the pain to end. I lost my family but if I can help prevent this from happening to others I will. It's hard to know your daughter is still alive, to see her and not be able to have the father daughter relationship that I should. Just because of someone's evil desires."

Tears welled up in his eyes as he spoke, the passion he spoke with said a lot. He was such a noble and humble man. The more he spoke the more of him you saw. Staring into his eyes you could see his soul, he was only good intentions. I had great doubt that there was a vile bone in his body.

"I lost it all. I can't remember all the details but certain things I see make me remember. I saw my daughter and I just knew it was her. As a father the connection never left. She looks just like her mum. No one in town remembers much. It's like they just blocked everything out.

"While we were in Canada, my wife's mother fell ill and from then she had changed. Before Madame Lenoiré fell sick, she was the sweetest thing. I remember when prior to Serena and I getting married, we came here to visit Paradise. We spent time with Serena's mother, Madame Lenoiré she was just so nice. She approved of me, she took me as her son and I asked for her daughter's hand in marriage and it was just the greatest moment.

"My wife's sister Marié Lennox and her husband Joseph Lennox also came down to visit since all the family was there. We all bonded, I felt like part of the family. When we returned to Montreal, Madame Lenoiré came up and spent some time with us before the wedding.

"All the family was there for the wedding, Marié and Joseph, and Serena's cousins; even their mother's caretaker Mariah was present. My brother met his wife at our wedding. Serena's mother went back with Mariah a month after the ceremony. A few years later Serena found out she was pregnant. It was the greatest feeling knowing that we were having a baby. When our daughter was born, there were many complications but she made it and just to hold her, to look at that little piece of me. We named her Serita, after her mother.

"Then a few years Serena's mum fell sick and she wanted to be with her mother. I felt it best for us to move here and start a new life; a better upbringing for our daughter as well. Jeanine Summers, was Serena's best friend and our daughter's godmother and her husband Bernard the godfather, they moved with us down here. Around the time we were moving, Marié and Joseph gave birth to the twins, Steven and Chauncé. I named them, they were our godchildren.

"Madame Lenoiré didn't make it too long, but before she died it's like she wasn't herself, something had taken over her and she wanted the twins. She made Marié and Joseph and the kids move down here but she passed the week they were due here. Strange things started happening. Mariah was acting weird. Then that Hank man was always around, every time he came around things got worse.

"A lot of stuff from there is sketchy, but I remember getting the call from Jeanine that my wife had died and my daughter was missing. When they told me that Serena had died, it killed me. Then my daughter was gone, no trace of her, it's like she just disappeared. I hoped that they were joking, I didn't believe it. I was miles away I don't know where I was or what I was doing but I remembered getting to the house and the yellow tape everywhere, Serena's blood was all over.

"I broke down crying, I just lay on the floor where her body had been found. While there I saw a hooded figure, dark cloak, I could have counted its ribs through the garments. I'd never seen anything like that before. Before it attacked me I looked at the face and I remembered seeing Anthony Hank.

"I forgot a lot of my life; but I always remembered my family and my friends. When I came home I remembered things slowly but by looking at certain items. The first thing I did was recover and secure the surveillance tapes from my office, it was well hidden. After a while Anthony walked through the door, and told me I was breaking and entering, and he called the police.

"When they arrived they treated me like they didn't know who I was. I was told I had no family, they drove me out of my home and told me that I was invading Anthony's house. Things like that went on for a while until I was committed to the mental institution, but before I was, I gave the tapes and all my records, files and documents to Father Monroe.

"From there my life went more downhill."

He continued speaking about the things, it was painful and heart breaking to hear him speak about his life. One thing was for sure, he remembered his wife and daughter and he insisted that she was alive. We continued talking for hours, we spoke of different things, but Father Monroe and I couldn't say any of what we knew about the curse. It hurt even more knowing that much and being unable to do anything.

We learned more about the great talking fire and Anthony's involvement. We also learned that Lilith had gotten hold of Madame Lenoiré, and that's why she was different, Anthony Hank was Lilith's footman, he had sold his family to her for all that he had earned, including Peter Thomas's life. He sold his soul and sacrificed his wife, two daughters and three sons. How could anyone bare to be so ruthless, seeing their own family killed just to earn riches and a life they hadn't worked for?

Chapter 8

The Speech

It was Monday the 27th, the day of the funeral. It crept upon me, the past few days had been a whirlwind of insanity. This day would be no ordinary day. People island wide would be attending. The turnout was expected to be more than eight hundred. Dignitaries, government officials and family and friends both local and from abroad who flew in were going to be present. Police from all the other constituencies had been asked to attend the funeral as the expected attendance superseded more than the Paradise Falls Police Department alone was capable of handling. Heightened security measures were in place, high profile attendees and emotional family, friends and others meant that this funeral could possibly become an easy target for crime or riots.

Thunder, lightning and torrential downpours ensued from the night before. Strong winds threatened as the community worked together preparing for the funeral. Wreaths were being made and brought in from all over. The town was crowded, vehicles and people all over, tying bows and ribbons on poles and columns all around the town. Flags all around the island were flown at half-mast, as respect was shown to those who had past and also their families and all affected by the incident.

Paradise: A Hidden Truth

The weather cleared up in time for the ceremony, I left home early to be there on time. Latricia and I went together. I was getting closer to her, we had grown, we bonded over time and we worked together. We saw the other every day. I was starting to like her, she grew on me, she was wise, pretty, confident, a sense of humour and an open mind. I didn't really notice how pretty she was until that day when I picked her up from her place. She was simple, didn't need much to look amazing, but that day I really saw her. I had always seen her only in ponytails, but today her hair was dropped and styled. Her eyes were a deep brown, but there was a beautiful light brown outline.

As I stare at her I got excited, I felt things I questioned but then I thought about how natural it all was. Her face was flawless as if airbrushed. Her lips pink as a spring rose. Her smile... her smile was just perfect. Everything was just amazing. Her skin a caramel chocolate shade, I never noticed her until now. I was turned on just looking at her. I was falling for her. As she walked to the car, her black dress a cut over her knees, sparkling in the sunlight. The material reflecting the rays as they bounced off her body. Her legs glistened below. Her sensuous shape, the curves... I rushed out of the car to open the door for her as she walked down the stairs in her heels. I marvelled at her as she drew nearer. The closer she got the more I noticed. I tried not to stare, but how could I avoid a sight so beautiful, so sexy, so magnificent?

She stood five feet eight inches tall and in the heels she was about three inches taller. As she stepped down I saw her thighs through the split of her dress, it run from her knees on both sides to her midsection and the fabric below complemented the dress. I longed to see more of her. I opened the door and walked over to her at the gate.

"You look rather ravishing today, might I take your hand?" as I spoke I outstretched my hand to her. She extended her hand to mine; I gently took her hand and kissed it, embracing her hand tenderly as I escorted her to the vehicle.

"Why thank you sir." She blushed, "Might I add that you look handsome yourself." She stare into my eyes, I felt the connection.

We drove over to the church, finding a parking close enough. As we got out, we held each other by hooking elbows, locking our arms. Intertwined as a securely knotted rope, we looked like a couple. We sat next to each other at the proceedings. It was a very emotional occasion. Family and friends of the victims, classmates, colleagues, teachers, it was complete turmoil and chaos. The mass lasted two and a half hours, it didn't seem like much. I noticed a strange woman in a black veil that stood out. I took pictures of her. Something about her made my skin crawl. I was uneasy. I pointed it out to Latricia, she had noticed her too. A few seats over, I noticed Peter eyeing the woman attentively. His eyes were fixated on her.

After the mass as we proceeded to the cemetery for the burial, I noticed the woman again, this time she was with Anthony Hank. There was another woman walking with them. I hadn't seen her around town. Peter was following closely behind them, something was going on. Latricia and I followed them; keeping them in eyes view, trailing carefully behind trying not to be noticed or to look too suspicious. They were up to something; the way they moved together seemed strange, staring intently at the hearse procession as they moved through the thick crowd of people. I remembered Anthony at the meeting wanting to have the funeral on unconsecrated ground, and the debate that ensued. What were they up to? Peter looked back at us and gave us a signal ushering us toward him. This was what he was referring to in the statement. They were after something and had to wait for the day of the burial in order to get it.

We went to meet up with him. Father Monroe was way ahead with the other Catholic heads: priests, bishops and deacons leading the procession along its way. Out of the blue a man in a white suit riding a white horse merged into the convoy finding himself right behind the policemen that were trailing the hearses and the families. Latricia, Peter and I ran along the side pavement to get further ahead. As we got to the front we noticed his eyes were two black holes, just empty. It was weird seeing something like that in a crowd so vast during broad daylight. Peter told us he was going up to warn Father Monroe. This was bigger than us.

He moved carefully to the front and walked along Father Monroe, giving him a hand signal. Father Monroe then raised his right hand and almost as if being controlled the Catholic heads reached into their garments and starting sprinkling holy water with their right hands while holding thuribles that contained burning incense, spreading clouds of light smoke. The man on the horse stopped immediately avoiding going further into the smoke. Then he just vanished, as if he got lost in the crowd. I wondered if anyone else was seeing what was taking place. I grew up knowing that the holy water and incense was used as cleansing and to ward off evil spirits.

We neared the gates to the cemetery and the veiled woman, Anthony and the mysterious woman all walked hastily trying to catch up to the hearses. The police had stopped allowing the hearses, Catholic heads and families to continue. That hindered them they had to stop. Those heading the procession entered into the gates, and then the police continued on marching leading the rest of the crowd into the gates. The veiled woman stopped and receded as this happened. She was at the service but couldn't enter the cemetery. Anthony Hank and the mysterious woman kept on walking. We got to the site of the burial and the crowd circled around the Catholic heads and the families.

The two of them seemed to try to get closer but the people were unmovable. Anthony looked furious. The priests consummated the funeral ritual by placing the coffins into their final resting places. As the coffins were lowered it was pure pandemonium, screams and cries were even louder and more forceful. Anthony and the strange woman had already left. It seemed like they had failed their mission. Their intentions were foiled by a religious army who had prepared for this. Things were getting more outlandish, while all that was going on was baffling, it was weird and wonderful.

After the funeral ceremony while the families, friends and mourners went back to the multipurpose centre where the reception was being held for refreshments and mingle, Latricia, Peter and I headed to the presbytery to meet up with Father Monroe. Curiosity filled us as we wondered what had just happened. When he began speaking, it was like the twilight zone. The lady in the veil was Lilith, she was real as daylight. The mysterious woman was Viola, another who had sold her soul and Hank, all of Lilith's followers. Devil worshipers who had come to finish what they started. Viola was the one who made the day of the accident; she was responsible for it all. She was the one who held the voodoo dolls. They came to claim the spirits, the last thing left of these bodies. They wanted to use the spirits of the victims as a bonus to their master, the man in white... the devil.

The days seemed to slowly crawl by, it seemed like an eternity. Though the memory of the incident that took place just three weeks ago had been planted into our memories, life had to go on. Things continued as normal as they could, it was now time for graduation. The event was re-planned to accommodate the recent losses suffered. It almost seemed to theme the life and times of the late Jeynna Seymouré. It was now Bianca Tate who had taken place of valedictorian. In the crowd I noticed Peter, there at the graduation ceremony.

Bianca was as stunning as a rose; she was the prettiest girl at school. Her long flowing black hair was like silk. Her ebony skin possessed a tender glow almost olive like. She was a younger darker version of Halle Berry with a slight resemblance to Dana Aaliyah Haughton. Her innocence showed in her face. Her eyes were a light hazel that resembled brown amber.

Paradise: A Hidden Truth

The event was subtle, but it was so sad but at the same time, it was our best. The proceedings went smoothly. It was now time for the anticipated high point-the valedictorian speech, given by Bianca Tate. She didn't show a hint of fear or anxiety. In fact, she was much relaxed. She was cheered and applauded as she made her way through the crowd and up to the stage. Peter gazed intently at her, that same twinkle in his eye. He never mentioned much about his daughter he just said he'd seen her around town a few times, never gave much detail. Looking at her I noticed a slight resemblance. Could it be that Bianca Tate was who he said his daughter was?

She began, "A warm and pleasant good evening to you all, and welcome to the graduation of the class of 2010. 'The undisputed academic warriors!' I came here with a pre-planned speech, but now is not the time for a reminder of our brilliance or capabilities, now is the time to address the issues at hand. As I stand here before you tonight; fellow classmates, parents and devoted staff, I see powerful people, conquerors, people who did their utmost best to assist in the upbringing, nurturing and educating of us the youth, the leaders of tomorrow.

"It is with great sincerity and respect that I speak on behalf of all of us who have yet to evolve into our elders. Our thanks and gratitude we share with you, not just for doing your jobs, but also for going out of your ways to protect us from the world— from ourselves. The bonds that unite us, the friendships, the helping hands that comfort us in our most desperate times of need.

"But now more than ever we have to appreciate what should be our top priorities: our family, our friends and our lives, our community... if we all come together it would be for the benefit and the betterment of us all. One family, one cry!" She stared blankly into the audience for a while; her eyes glistened with the presence of held back tears. Then she continued, "I know I sound like a desperate politician trying to secure my position, to satisfy my hungry thirst, but I stand here before you as a mere teenager, as a child-your child, a cry for help trying to reach a people," her voice breaks as she delivers her heartfelt thoughts-the truth; struggling to maintain her composure, to hold back her emotions.

The crowd obviously deeply moved at this point listened attentively as this remarkable sixteen year old gave the speech of a leader-a senior. Her maturity spoke for itself, it was unbelievable. Her resonance was of someone who had been around-a younger Maya Angelou.

"I know you're all wondering where this is going, but look around you at our changing world. Look at the parents of today: those who still require parenting themselves. Our young men, instead of being the men that they should be, choose to live life on the edge; drugs, guns, crime, sex, gangs, violence. It's not only our young men; it's our young women and our adults. Who is to blame for this? Society? Maybe bad parenting... how about the media? Yes, all these are only some of the contributing factors, but how about blaming ourselves-instead of pointing fingers? Any child has freewill, freedom to opinions, choices and decisions. However, it's the ones we decide upon that make all the difference.

"We will often find people who blame 'parenting', but is that really it? No! It's not upbringing, or where you come from.

It's mentality. It's the need to be, the desire for attention, the craving for notice. Our cry for help, a cry so loud yet it is silenced by our blindness and our ignorance. We can never move forward if we close our eyes and turn the other way. What we accomplish compared to what we need to accomplish. The contrast is as greatly obvious as that of day and night. Yet we fail to notice what needs to be done. Tonight, I know I have strayed from the annual graduation ritual, but I ask; what is it that you want?!"

As she steps down, the uncertainty of applause is conked out by my standing ovation, which is followed by all present. As usual, the need to be a follower is observed in this chronic exhibit of limitations. Overcome with shock Bianca burst into an affectionate display of tears, while obviously forcing a smile to masque her true emotion. She finally manages to muster a convincing smile after repetitiously trying with constant difficulties… such a captivating beauty. Then a sudden cloud of graduation caps filled the open sky, reminding us that the graduation ceremony had come to an end. She was well spoken, pleasant, her tone and her serenity, that calm and soft approachable disposition reminded me of Peter.

Bianca had been raised by a biracial couple. Her mother Soko, was from Japan and her father Hassan was Egyptian. Anthony Hank had always visited the family; I never really thought much of any of it until now. It started to make sense to me. He had taken over that case and he acted as the social worker assigned to the family. I never noticed it until now. It didn't even cross my mind that Bianca was adopted, there was a lot more to this. I would put my life on it that she didn't know that these were not her parents either.

After the ceremony I went to Peter, trying not to raise the subject. He had tissues wiping his eyes; he was well dressed in a black suit and tie. When he saw me he just smiled and started crying even more, but tears of joy as well as sadness. It was a bittersweet cry. That was the only explanation: Bianca Tate was really Serita Thomas, Peter's daughter who was said to be missing. How could anyone have missed that? I remembered the curse and Anthony's involvement in the whole thing started to become more disturbing. It was puzzling. Why did they take his daughter and how did the adoption documents not show that Peter was her father? What was it about Bianca they needed? Why did they hide her identity and why did Peter not reveal? Maybe he knew something more.

I wasn't sure of any of it but it was the first thing that came to mind. I had to think of something, a way to get the DNA of both Peter and Bianca and see if my speculation was right. I spoke to Peter that night and bought him dinner and invited along Latricia and Father Monroe. Seeing it was a huge event I know the crowd would have been vast and mixed. Nobody would think much of seeing us all in the same place. There was nothing wrong and we all acted casually.

I bought Bianca a bottle of non-alcoholic champagne from the bar, and held a toast for her. I got her cup afterwards and secured it. I told Father Monroe of my intentions. I let Latricia know that I needed to have some items processed for DNA samples. I didn't tell her the exact reason, nor did I tell her who the samples were from. I labelled the packets 'A' for Peter and 'B' for Bianca. The night went well, and incident free.

*   *   *

That morning I got up to a rude awakening. The days past seemed like something straight out a Stephen King novel. I wondered if it was real, but the daily news programs were there as usual to replay all the horror stories, while it briefly touched the good. She was right, we are living in a changing world, and not a soul seems to take notice or accept the changes present and noticeably obvious. It's as if we've shut our eyes, pretending that all is well- knowing that it had not been for years. Did it really have to take the eyes of a teenager to point out a crisis so belligerently hostile, veiled by a fictitious innocence produced by ourselves? It took a teenager, to remind us of the ever so present and sturdy increase of crime - of violence, just complete and utter disparity. It was surreal, a movie script. Now that it was pointed out, it became a reality now multidimensional, rather than the one-dimensional comic strip we had so profoundly carved in our heads. We had been slapped in the face by the untimely problems of the real world, of real life. We had neglected the presence of those hauntings; we had turned our backs on them like dilapidated rundown fortresses.

Something needed to be done. Action was now overdue and we failed to accept responsibility for a problem we had inherited, and provoked. Now was the time to answer our call, to stamp out the problem, eliminate the enemy-but how? I felt stupid; I was one of those people who failed to do anything. Even I had turned my back, and closed my eyes. I created the illusion, a constant reminder that all was well. For days I punished myself for being so naïve, so blind. The truth hit me. All this time, all these things I had seen, all was starting to unfold.

With all that going on I headed to work hoping to hear word from the lab, hoping that the results were in and something was found. As I walked to my office, I noticed Latricia hurrying into the front door with a blue envelope in her hand. She gestured me over to my office, we got in and she closed the blinds. She looked stunned.

"Shaun, I got back the report, but I got a call from the person running the test and they told me that Subject A and B matched each other and that A was the paternal match for B. I was a bit confused. You had a paternity test order done?"

"Yes, I wasn't sure of what exactly I expected I just had a hunch on something so I decided to do some investigative work. I should have told you. I just didn't want to jump the gun with this."

"D-D-Do you have kids? Are you a father?"

"Wha-What? No! That's crazy, I mean not that I don't want to be someday but I mean if I were a father I'd wear it on my sleeve. I love kids yes, but I have none of my own... I suppose what I am saying is the test wasn't mine."

She looked relieved; she let out a slight breath of reprieve. "Oh... Oh I was just wondering." Her face was flush, she was blushing. "So... who was the test for then...?"

"Well it was for Peter Thomas but he doesn't know I had it done he doesn't know I took the samples either."

"Peter? Wait, um what is going on? Peter has a child? Do you know this child? I thought his child had died or was missing."

"Well he was right about his daughter still being alive. We all know who this child is too."

"We do. Wait, we do? I do? Do I?"

I laughed she seemed befuddled. "Yes Latricia, we do. That night at the graduation I noticed something in Peter that I had seen every time he spoke of his daughter still being alive. That look, the conviction, the twinkle."

"His daughter was at the graduation?"

"His daughter was the graduation, she was the valedictorian."

"What are you saying Shaun? I'm a bit confused."

"Well, it's simple actually. Well not really, it's actually a lot more complicated. At the graduation as she collected her awards, I noticed Peter's elation, like he knew something, he just had that look. At first I thought it weird, but I remembered the look, and then it hit me: that's his daughter. After a while I thought about it and thought that Soko and Hassan Tate were her parents. So there was no way, but then I really thought about it like really and conjured up this little plan. Anyway, just to cut to the chase, the thing is Bianca Tate, is really Serita Thomas, Peter's daughter."

"Whoa, Shaun... This is a bit much. I mean, how come if he suspected he never mentioned it?"

"Um, his reputation around town as the village crazy person... I doubt he'd do anything to create more confusion. Seeing the way he spoke of his daughter he obviously loves her, and he cares... cares too much even to try to let his suspicions be known, just to avoid ruining her life.

"Wow. I don't think I'd ever be able to. I mean if I were a mother and... I don't know." She paused for a while, as if in deep contemplation. "Maybe if I were in that position, I would do the same coming to think of it. She's just a child"

"You ever noticed that Peter is very open and honest? He is also very protective."

"Yes, I do, he is humble and modest, a great character, his humility is beyond me, how can he be so calm and nice."

"It's because it's who he is. He never lost all of himself."

"Wow... I mean... I don't know. I have nothing but the utmost respect for this man. Like, how could you go through life balancing all that and still maintaining your sanity while everyone else thinks of you as crazy? He must be really strong, not many people would manage that even I'd buckle under the pressure. It seems like he's been cursed."

These words... She noticed it. She said it not meaning anything but if only she knew that's exactly what it was. She was so right about it but had no idea. Things lingered in my head. Anthony Hank was involved and I needed to know what part he played. I wanted his head for whatever it was. He ruined the lives of so many people, of this man who was made to live miserably. He lost his family, and had to live life knowing that his daughter was alive, knowing who she was and not being able to be that father figure to her. Not being able to be there for the special moments, no mother around and having to watch his child raised by complete strangers. How could he have managed all that and keep such perfect equilibrium? I needed to go to Father Monroe with this, I took Latricia with me.

I called ahead this time letting him know that we wanted to drop by. He gave the okay and I was more than eager to get there.

Chapter 9

Facing Reality

We got to the presbytery an hour and a half later, after grabbing lunch at this fancy Japanese restaurant down in the centre of town called Suki Hana. When we got there Peter had already arrived. It was hard to look at him without feeling guilt, pain and sadness, not saying anything about Bianca's true identity. We couldn't. Father Monroe led us to a small viewing room; at the front was a full entertainment system. Peter reached for the shelf where he took something and handed it to Father Monroe who walked up to the shelf holding the television and other electronic players. It was a video cassette; he took it out of its casing and popped it in the VCR player.

"This is the first time that we will be reviewing the tape, well all of us but Peter." Father Monroe announced. "It is the surveillance tape from the night of the disappearance of his daughter and the murder of his wife."

"I don't remember much about the tape, it's like most of my memory just washed away the day Hank invaded my home." Peter added.

The tape started, there were ten small windows monitoring different areas of the house: the front gate and yard, the front door and path to the gate, the entrance hall and stairwell to the second floor, the kitchen and dining room, the study, library and powder room door, the top floor showing two adjacent doors on either side of the length of the hall and a door to the end to the master bedroom, a camera in the master bedroom, one in Serita's room, a camera that gave a panoramic view of the full backyard and house from a pole overshadowing the back fence, one for the basement and another in the attic. At first all the activity seemed normal. Then someone appeared at the front gates. It was Viola, the woman from the funeral.

Serita was playing up in her room while Serena was in the kitchen preparing a meal. Viola reached for the buzzer, Serena walked over to the intercom and spoke, the audio kicked in. It was crystal clear. She was asking who it was while looking into the monitor mounted into the intercom. Viola was their replacement housekeeper, after their regular had disappeared mysteriously. She opened the gate and allowed her in. A few moments later Viola had walked up to the front door where Peter's wife stood waiting to let her in. She rung the door bell and Serena double-checked, looking into the peephole before letting her in.

She opened the door and welcomed Viola in. Viola walked through, heading to the powder room. While she was doing that, Mrs. Thomas went to check on Serita before heading back downstairs with her. They were laughing and cooking together, joking, speaking and playing as they cooked. They looked so happy; they were also baking a cake, probably preparing for a special occasion.

I saw Peter out the corner of my eyes, a smile was on his face as he watched his family. He started crying, tears rolled down his face as he cried silently, trying hard not to breakdown. He had that look in his eyes again as he watched the tape. He wiped his face, his expression had changed. I focused my attention on the screen again.

Viola was coming out of the powder room; she had changed her clothes and headed down to the basement where she started on her chores. She was mouthing something as she walked; silent words and her hands were moving strangely. What was she doing? Peter's wife and daughter continued their bonding while Viola went upstairs into the room closest to the master bedroom. She opened her arms widely and brought them back together outstretched in front of her. Something was in her hand, a small black round marble or something. She placed it on the bed and it slowly floated up to the ceiling. She then went into the master bedroom and placed her left hand on the bed, a black wisp of smoke went up to the ceiling, its movement was animated.

Meanwhile, downstairs Mrs. Thomas and Serita were placing the baking trays into the oven and started washing the dishes. They then headed out to the dining room setting the table for three. While they were doing this Viola had joined asking Mrs. Thomas if they needed help, to which Mrs. Thomas responded no telling Viola to take a rest before joining them for dinner. So thoughtful of her I thought as I watched. After a while they sat to dinner and Serita offered to say grace before they enjoyed the meal.

After dinner, Serita and her mom climbed up the stairs in the foyer heading up to their rooms. Serena led her daughter to the room kissing her before heading to hers. They disappeared from the camera's focus for a while and then emerged a few moments later dressed in their pyjamas, looking refreshed. Mrs. Thomas knocked on Serita's door and Serita had allowed her in, they started playing again. They then headed over to Serita's bed where Mrs. Thomas was tucking her in then reading her a bedtime story; it was so pleasant how they were together. Following the story, Serita asked about her dad, and her mom reassured her that he would be back soon.

They then prayed and mom stayed around until Serita fell asleep. When Serita was fast asleep she kissed her forehead and headed toward the door, turning off the light as she exited the room. She returned to her room and lay in her bed where she kissed a picture on her bed stand. She went back down to check on Viola who was preparing to leave. They bid each other 'good night', Viola left. She made sure Viola had cleared the property then turned off the lights inside the house and headed back to her room. The phone rang and she answered. Her face lit up as she mentioned her husband's name. It was Peter calling.

After the phone call, she clapped the lights off and went to sleep. The tape was fast forwarded a few hours later, to 01:00. Someone was seen walking in Serita's room while they were both still fast asleep. The figure wasn't made out until coming in the direct view of the camera. It was Anthony Hank. He waved his hand over Serita and she became as stiff as a board. He then took out a silver orb and they both just disappeared from the room. It was puzzling. He and Serita had vanished.

Peter's face was angry. He was crying even more. His hands were opening and closing profusely. Then his fists were balled up. Trying hard to compose himself he managed to simmer down, still quietly shedding tears.

The tape forwarded a little bit more, at exactly 03:00 a dark creature was in the bedroom that Viola had entered. It was tall and lanky. It had no eyes, nose or any other features, just a blank face. I noticed it from the book that Father Monroe had been using to help me with the things I had been seeing. It was a phatom. Its purpose was to steal humans for its master, then return the body to the master who would then take certain parts of the being it had stolen to make a totem for evil. The master would write down the instructions and inscribe them unto a dark black crystal, and at a certain time, the demon would be released. It moved about obtusely, its body moving in different directions like a static animation. It's back bent and it leaned forward; it moved almost like a crab, but walking backwards.

It entered into Serita's room heading to her bed, but nothing was there. It then disappeared. While this was happening at the same time a thick smoke of grey, white and black emerged from the ceiling of the master bedroom. It went to the floor where it started changing into a person from the feet up. It was Lilith. She then placed her black veil over her head, flickered something and she changed into Madame Lenoiré. She then walked up to the bed, staggering and stumbling knocking things over as she moved. The noise had woken up Serena, who woke up alarmed and stunned. She called out asking who was there and then her eyes stare at the figure. She called out, 'mom', then pulled away sticking closer to the head of the bed. She let out, 'mom, you're dead'.

The figure moved closer to the bed, floating above the ground. Its body bent over leaning forward, stretched as if made of rubber until it got its face close enough to Serena. It then stretched its hands, almost in an instant it had become Lilith again, she looked like a demon, and her hands became long claw like things with sharp nails. Her face was distorted with holes in it and red eyes. Serena was screaming loudly. The creature then reached out placing her claws into Serena's eyes gouging them out. She was claiming her soul. She then swallowed them and dragged Serena down to the foyer, where she cut her up into pieces using her claws. Blood was everywhere.

She then disappeared with a bright white blue spark display with particles of red, then a billow of smoke and then everything was gone. All that remained were the mangled pieces of what used to be Mrs. Serena Thomas. The time forwarded to 07:00 the phone was heard ringing. Peter's voice was over the answering machine saying he would call back a bit later after his meeting, or the next morning since he was in Belgium and the time was different. 08:45 the phone rang again. It was a female voice this time announcing herself as Jeanine, saying she didn't get the regular wakeup call so she was calling to check. Serena's cell phone rang, and then rang out, this happened a few times. 09:15 the phone rang again with the same female voice, Jeanine now a bit worried announced she would be coming over to the house and asking if the maid wasn't home to answer the call.

10:02, a car drove through the gate and up to the roundabout at the front of the house. A female was seen exiting the vehicle at the front lifting up one of the bricks under the front mat where she took out a key. She opened the front door and fell to the ground, screaming and crying at what she saw, she run back to her car. Looking lost... dazed and confused, she drove away in a hurry, tires burning as she sped off on the cobblestone driveway. She disappeared from the cameras view. 10:53 she returned with a troop of emergency vehicles.

She stood outside as they worked, on her cell phone trying to call somebody. Eventually she got the person, it was Peter. She was calling him, frantically delivering the message informing him of what had happened. She said it was no prank, still crying she mentioned the details of what the emergency response team had told her that might have taken place.

Peter was no longer looking at the screen, he was crying profusely and his face was covered by his hands. As the footage of the call showed, he burrowed his face into his laps. Latricia had noticed and went over to try to console him. He said he was okay. She got him some tissue and patted his back and he let off a gentle smile.

On screen again, a few hours later after everyone had left, a hired cab drove up to the front of the house. Peter was seen exiting in his business attire, rushing up to the house rushing through all the police tape. He entered through the door and turned on the lights, as he looked he fell to the ground, blood stains were everywhere. He staggered to where the pieces of his mangled wife were found earlier and lay in the spot. He stayed there for a moment. He then left and went to the study, where he watched the tapes and copied what he saw. He watched in horror and anguish as his daughter was taken and his wife slain. He saw all the things that happened. After watching the tape he left the house with two copies, on one he had written 'Father Monroe' and on the other, 'Paradise Falls P.D.'

When he returned to the house the following day, that's when he saw the black figure hovering around his home, he followed it, parts of the film were blacked out, and chunks were missing. Then Anthony Hank was there and the police came arresting Peter for trespassing. Looking at the date on the tape it was a week later. What had happened? It seemed like the spell was already cast, the memory spell.

We spent hours going over everything, replaying pieces of the tape as we did. Peter spoke about what happened... he started remembering things. He spoke about taking the tape to Father Monroe and him telling Father Monroe that he believed that his mother-in-law had died after their wedding very shortly after her return to Paradise. Father Monroe confirmed and said he knew but couldn't say anything going along with the orders from his superiors. They knew that Lilith was in Paradise and she had killed and assumed the identity of Madame Lenoiré. Things only became more complicated, more confusing. What we saw, the things that Peter had revealed and Father Monroe confirming everything. The atmosphere started to change slowly, like there was a surge in time. We felt light headed. Peter had remembered the details of his life. Had the spell been broken? We had to wait and see as the days carried on. Only time would tell.

*   *   *

Paradise: A Hidden Truth

Learning that bit of information from Father Monroe about Madame Lenoiré, it was a lot to process, so much to sort out. She had died days after coming back from the wedding and this Lilith woman was responsible for her death and had taken her place. Seeing the surveillance recordings of Peter's home was a revelation.

I had to also find out all there was to about Mr. Peter Alexandre Thomas. It's like any prior memories of him before he was labelled Crazy Pete had been erased from all who knew him. I dug up old files from the library, newspaper articles and anything else I could find. I called every agency for any documents I could on him. The Department of Statistics and Public Records was where I found the bulk of the information I needed. What I found out was a lot more than I expected. As I got information I documented it and wrote up a sort of profile and back story of the man who was Peter Alexandre Thomas.

*　　*　　*

Peter Alexandre Thomas was twenty eight years old when he moved to Paradise Falls ten years earlier from Quebec, Canada with his wife Serena and their five year old daughter Serita. His wife was born and raised in Paradise Falls, and was the daughter of Madame Lenoiré Bontoft, who suggested that they come to Tesoro. While in Canada he taught at the Université de Montréal as it was called by the francophone. He had also earned his PhD in Law and was a lawyer at a very prestigious law firm; his own law firm that he handed over to his older brother Adrian when he made the move to Paradise.

When he first moved to the island, he worked for the government of Tesoro as well as other islands and had earned his position and status as a diplomat. He had earned a name for himself worldwide and here in Tesoro. He had accomplished great things and made great contributions to the country's growth and to the other neighbouring islands. He even helped boost the economy and introduced new methods of construction, new businesses, new and improved agricultural advances and created a more sound law system. Paradise Falls just like many other communities had benefited greatly from his devotion and his dedication to improving all areas and creating better measures.

Things were going really great for him until the disappearance of his daughter and the mysterious death of his wife while he was away on a business trip in Belgium. He was approving a deal for the Tesoro's Trafalgar International Airport to become the first hub on the western seaboard for Quake Air, the national airline of Belgium. The day after finalising the deal while in his hotel room in Brussels, Belgium's capital city he received a call relaying the news to him. With a week left on his trip he cut it short and booked himself a chartered flight back home. The ten hour flight seemed to last an eternity.

The contents of the call had kept replaying as he broke down, unable to control himself. Distraught and filled with disbelief by the unfortunate news that he had lost his wife and that his daughter was missing had changed everything. To him his world had come to an end. He spent years building a life for his family, and they were taken from him. He broke down crying. A grown man brought to tears, but no one could have imagined how intense this must have been on him.

No pain compared to the pain, anguish and agony he felt; he felt empty and hollow. His wife, his partner of years, more than a decade and his daughter, a piece of him were both gone. He remembered how hard the pregnancy was for his wife and now it all meant nothing. He hoped that he would get back home and find that it was just a joke, that the call would turn out to be a cruel prank played on him by Jeanine Summers, his wife's best friend who called to relay the message. Jeanine was not only his wife's best friend; she was also Serita's godmother and babysitter who moved from Canada with them as a friendly gesture to the family.

She was very well off and always dreamed of living in the Caribbean, when she found out they were moving, she and her husband Jonathan and their three children Stephan, Lynthia and Tchad moved with them. They built a home right next to the Peters' residence and bought property in town where they opened a few businesses including a flower shop, an antique shop and a supermarket where they created many jobs and provided goods and services at low costs and also a market for local farmers to sell their produce.

Anything was better than finding his wife and daughter gone. He would give anything to have another chance at life with his family. He never wanted to leave Montreal, but his wife's mother insisted after the birth of their daughter they come back to Paradise. He did reluctantly, but he did because his wife didn't want to say no to her mother and he understood that but now they were gone.

He got back to Paradise at five the following morning. The first and only thing that was on his mind was getting back to the place that had been home to him. This was no longer home he thought as his family was no more. He got to the house and yellow police tape was everywhere. Most of the officers had already left. It had been more than fifteen hours since the body had been discovered.

*   *   *

We needed to know more about the spells cast, about the people involved and the depth of their participation. We had to go about it carefully and strategically. Father Monroe had referred me to a lady and told me that he had set up a meeting with her, a Miss Linda Wright. I had heard so much about her, and Latricia had always spoken so highly of her. She said that a lot of what she learned about the town of Paradise and Tesoro was from Linda. All the books she had studied about the history were given to her by Linda. Linda also showed her some of the locations of these happenings and the markings left behind by the Amerindians and the previous inhabitants of Tesoro. She also found a lot of information from the local libraries and from conducting interviews with some of the elders that were still alive on the island.

I was excited, I had heard so much about Linda, read so much about her. I even read her books. I never had the opportunity of meeting her personally but I had been to her seminars with Latricia and she also conducted training sessions at town hall for town professionals. She was very loved by the residents, but she also had many who did not like her. In just a few more days, my dream would come true. Finally I would meet the legendary Linda Wright.

Chapter 10

Ego over Issues

"Let us continue with this bloody meeting, I have better things to do and this… it's ridiculous that I have to sit here and put up with this just cause some little girl chose to play Martin Luther! I have things to tend to" Mr. Anthony Hank was heard exclaiming with a bellow.

"How ignorant and self-centred you are, it's not Bianca's fault that any of our heads were so far up our asses that we never took the necessary steps! What is it Anthony, is it because you were not the one to bring up the matter?! Why does everything have to be about you? I'm sick of it and I'm sick of you!" Ms. Joanne Eugene screamed back at the top of her lungs.

"Okay now, stop it right there that's enough the both of you! This is the most petty display of immaturity thus far Mr. Hank," said Mrs. Judith Sayers. "It seems like every time somebody else gives light on an issue, or has an idea that's beneficial to us all it angers you, and that's all the time. When have you ever contributed anything of substance to this Committee?"

Hank was eager to reply "You're such a repugnant bitch Judy, and you know what, I quit this committee!"

This had turned into another Hank knows best things. Mr. Hank had moved back here from Seattle after living there for fifteen years. He said that he worked for the U.S. Congress while living in the United States. He was extremely ill tempered, and arrogant, a bit of a snob.

He heaved out of the conference room obviously heated. The murmurs had now erupted into a wave of laughter and rejoice. Little did he know that that was the best thing he had to offer to our board and its members. His outrageously belligerent outbursts and rants had gone on forever; this had turned into a routine, a script. Now the oaf was finally gone.

Cheers filled the room, a well expected reaction. The meeting had to go on, with or without one less distraction. The mood in the room had changed drastically, it was a more effective environment, and the meeting went smoothly from there.

"I'm so sorry," Ms. Eugene continued, "I just lost it, Hank always has this air of arrogance about him." She seemed a bit red, after all it was the first time we'd ever seen her upset.

"It's okay," we responded in unison. She was the only one apart from me who finally stood up and actually found the courage to put Hank in his place, a well-deserved treat.

*   *   *

"We really need to clear the air on these issues," stated Mrs. Sayers "we never before saw the reason to touch base on what was brought up by Miss Bianca. It's embarrassing to more than just an extent, it's ludicrous. As much as it lingered and bothered us all, we never ate out of our own plates, instead we played it no mind, and now it has come back to haunt us tenfold."

*   *   *

"Shaun! Hurry up! You're going to be late! You don't want to keep that young lady waiting on you." I heard mom's voice shouting over the music and the water as I showered.

I always showered with music, it was soothing. Singing along with the music as I scrubbed, I had already shaved my face and trimmed my hair. "Mum, I don't have to pick her up for another two hours; it's only nine in the morning. I have to get her by eleven."

"Young man, it's never in good light when a woman is left waiting. I know she's looking forward to your little date. I remember your father and I's official first date. He came ten minutes earlier and I was already looking out the window half an hour before. He took me to one of my favourite places, the Golden Falls. He sure did his research."

"Yup I sure did, and we were married six years later... good things came out of us being together. The greatest thing was you son!" My dad's voice had joined in.

They continued reminiscing on the times they had. I had never heard my father speak that way. He was always the tough one, but hearing him talking about dates and love... I was taken back. It was different, I was actually proud. I'd never heard him speak of the day I was born like that. When I was finally out of the shower I scurried over to my room hoping not to be seen, almost tripping over when I noticed I had forgotten my bath towel in my room. What an embarrassment it would be if my parents saw me running cupping my crotch as I run across the hallway. As I run I overheard my mom and dad still continuing their reminiscing. They heard me running across the floors overhead.

"He forgot his towel again," I heard my father saying to mum, "I think we need a towel stack mounted in the bathroom, or even a linen closet."

Mum laughed, agreeing with dad, "He's his father's son." I heard her reply with a chortle.

I could have gone a few more years going without knowing that tidbit. I laughed. My parents actually were really funny people. I got to my room, trying to decide what to wear, casual, formal, so much to decide. I threw on a white vest, topped up with a long-sleeved blue and white shirt with vertical stripes and put on a black pair of jeans with my black low rise sneakers. I was never really one for fashion; I always dressed to feel comfortable being mindful of the occasion. I checked myself once more in the full body mirror hanging on the back of my bedroom door. I thought I looked good enough and ready to go.

I walked downstairs and mum and dad waited for my entry. "Awww there's my baby boy. You look so handsome, you've grown so much. You're not the same little boy we nursed and nurtured. You're a man now. They never thought you'd make it past seven, but look, you've surpassed that. I always had faith, I hoped and prayed and did all that I could. I had never seen your father more worried. Everyone was concerned about you growing up. Look at you now." mom said looking at me with a warm smile. "You look just like your father." She said turning to him.

"Yup! That's my boy!" Dad exclaimed proudly. "Have fun out there and take good care of that young lady, I know we brought you up the right way and you've always done your best, so I am confident you know just what to do. Always remember that we love you son. You're very special to us." Wow, what had gotten into dad?

"Thanks mom, and dad. Dad, I've not seen this side of you much. I love you both. I don't say this enough but thank you, for being the best parents and for always doing the best and showing me right from wrong." As I spoke I had flashbacks of me growing up and my parents doing activities with me, fishing with dad and going boating. The memories I would cherish forever were the times spent with my loved ones, my family and friends. I felt tears welling up in my eyes. "Oh, look at the time", I said pretending to look at the invisible watch on my wrist! I tried to avoid them noticing my eyes but I saw that they were also emotional. "I love you guys, see you all later on." Kissing them both and hugging them as I left.

I got into my car and headed over to Latricia's place. As I drove my reggae playlist was on the car stereo. This was our first break from anything weird, a break from work; a day to have fun and enjoy each other's company without any extras or third or fourth wheels, just Latricia and me. I was excited, a whole weekend together. I had planned something special, something different, seeing as she loved the ocean and travelling, this was the perfect idea.

Arriving at her house fifteen minutes later I walked to the front door and knocked three times. Her mother answered the door.

"Oh, you must be Shaun, it's so nice to finally meet you. Michelle will be down in a few."

"Thank you Mrs. Moore, it's a pleasure" I said while handing her a small present.

"A true gentle man... Michelle has spoken so highly of you. Her last boyfriend was a jerk! Some old snob from the Hills!"

Just then Latricia walked down the stairs, "Mom! Oh my, did you really have to?" she said timidly. Her sister Tessa was walking behind her with a brush in her hand.

"I'm only being honest honey..." her mom replied.

"Mummy does have a point Triscia." Tessa added with a bright smile on her face. "I couldn't stand him; he was so disgusting and obnoxious. At times I just wanted to beat his face in with a baseball bat." She added tauntingly, laughing as she spoke. "Hey Shaun, aren't you looking all cute and stuff for Latty, you look nice!"

"Are you guys being serious right now?" Latricia asked still blushing as if embarrassed. "Come on Tessa, get off it... let's not talk about jerks. Might I remind you of Andrew Johnson? You're still dating him. Besides Shaun and I are just good friends."

"Well you've all got valid points." Mr. Moore added walking through the front door. "A bunch of jerks! Finally someone decent." He added fuelling the fire. "Hey Shaun, how are your folks? I haven't been past there in such a long time... it's been a week I reckon."

"He's such a clown!" they all said in unison.

"I try my best." He said with a bellowing laugh. "You guys best get going, traffic up to the city is building up rather quickly."

"I agree! I'll see you guys later!"

"It was a pleasure meeting you all." I said as we walked out the door.

They had all come to the porch to wave goodbye.

We headed to the car; I opened the door for her as usual. She smiled and sat down. She was glowing. The more I saw of her, the prettier she looked. I closed the door and went over to the driver's side.

"Shaun, you look so sexy today. Changed a few things I see. I'm liking them, not that I don't find you sexy at other times, it's just a change seeing you out of the formal setting." She seemed nervous as she spoke.

"Thank you, you're pretty as usual."

"Aw Shaun, thanks." She said kissing me on the cheek.

"You're welcome. Your family is so cool, you guys are hilarious."

"They're crazy is what they are. So where are we headed?

"It's a surprise... I'm amazed that Tessa didn't tell you."

"She knew? That little bugger! I am so going to get her."

We drove all the way up to the north of the island, a forty five minute drive. The time was spent chatting and exchanging jokes and stories and remembering the past few days. Driving over to the bay, we entered unto a small lot and there sat a yacht docked at a small port. There was a band playing live music and the guide welcomed us, leading us on board the yacht. There was live entertainment, fire dancers and other performers. I knew that Latricia enjoyed the arts so I planned this whole thing for her. She had never been on a yacht before but had always said that it was her dream to one day go sailing as the most she'd done in the ocean was swim.

One of the entertainers came to take Latricia to get a swimsuit of her choice. I intended to take her swimming as well. She was smiling and blushing. As they left I gave the crew the rest of the details. I changed into my shorts and kept my vest on, taking off my shoes and placing them in the locker. Latricia and the lady returned, she was all dressed in a black two piece swim suit. Her body was so sexy; I couldn't keep my eyes off her. We went to the top deck where we stood on the ledge as the boat left the dock. She was so excited, yet nervous as this was her first experience sailing. We sailed out of the bay heading west around the island. It was so beautiful. I had been on boats before, but I'd never been on this side of the island on a boat before.

Latricia and I were closer, holding each other as we sailed going in a south westerly direction. The dancers came to the top of the deck performing a few routines for us, and then led us back downstairs to the dining area. There was a nicely set table directly in the centre of the dining room, placing for two directly across from each other. Scented candles on the table since it was only early afternoon, the windows were blacked out. Bottles of her favourite champagne sat on a bucket of ice on a table next to where we sat. She was speechless. She was so happy she kissed me. She expressed that nobody had ever done anything like it for her. As the food was served, we sailed passed the twin peaks and docked in the middle of the ocean where we got a better view of the scenery.

We ate our lunch and chatted with each other. This was such a beautiful moment not only for her but for me as well. It was so magnificent. I never expected it to be this relaxing and wonderful. When we were done eating we headed back to the top deck where there was a spa setting for the two of us. Masseurs were waiting for us. As we lay on the massage tables we watched dolphins swimming and playing in the bay close to the twin peaks. Latricia was even more excited, she was eager to go swimming with the dolphins.

After our massages were done, we went swimming and had someone take us diving and exploring the reefs. We got back on-board the vessel and continued sailing on along the coast going to the south and back up the other side towards Paradise Falls. The day had gone exceptionally well. Before docking at the main jetty down at the bay in Paradise Falls, she kissed me, this time it was even more passionate. We embraced each other. I felt myself getting turned on. Her body pressed upon mine, the feeling was so intense. Caressing every inch of her body as we kissed, it was the perfect conclusion to a great day.

I dropped her home that evening at about 8:30 and rushed home. I was excited. The adrenaline rush had been one like none other. When I got to the house my parents were watching a movie together. I greeted them and headed up to my room. I decided to call Jimmy and let him know what was happening, as I had always kept him updated with all the new developments. He joked about it and said that I was falling in love... If that's what love felt like, I didn't mind. He mentioned to me that he was considering coming down to stay with us for a while, his parents were coming to visit he'd come and just stay a bit longer. I was even more excited, my big brother and partner in crime and I would be back together again.

Turning on the television there were emergency warnings of a tropical depression with the possibility of becoming a storm. We were expecting it to make landfall in three days. The weather had already changed dramatically. The winds were strong and people were preparing their storm shutters and building sand walls. Schools had been closed due to the inclement weather, shelters around town had already opened and people from the town as well as surrounding areas were already registering for spaces and others had already moved in. The sea was already coming up past the shoreline, and unto some roads. Flooding had begun in some areas as the rains became heavier. Being close to the ocean had its advantages, but there were also many disadvantages faced.

Chapter 11

The Storm

The season was slowly coming to an end. The wet season had crept upon our feeble village. The atmosphere was relatively tense as the villagers made their annual hurricane preparations. Though the weather was horrid throughout the year, every summer brought some of the most torrential weather patterns as the island was located in the Tropical Climate Zone. Torrential downpours lingered, and threatened the very livelihood of the people of Paradise Falls. I hurried to get some supplies in preparation for the approaching hurricane. The wind tore through the village, what used to be whispers had turned into howling. The lightning struck; it was unlike anything I had seen before. I was amazed at the beauty of it all, awestruck by the change of nature.

I dashed through the double doors at the convenient store, what a relief it was to be inside and warm again. It was organised chaos and with the Christmas season quickly approaching people were everywhere-literally packed like sardines, except for the numerous displays of shopping carts. I hated shopping, and I hated crowds even more. The ongoing chit chatter of the shoppers was like the buzzing of a million bees, never-ending. I scurried to grab what I came in for, cleaning supplies, some food items, batteries, candles and of course novels, as I had gone through my entire collection of Stephen Kings. Oh he is a genius!

As I prowled through the aisles gathering items from my list, I thought that I caught a glimpse of something odd right at the corner of my eye. It didn't quite register, so I continued going down my list. I got to the household items and I saw the same mysterious mist-like figure just slowly hovering through the aisle. I thought it was maybe from the temperature mixture from the heat of the central air system and the cold from outside. I kept about my business, just as I was reaching to the shelf to grab a few packets of candles the mist swooped down through the aisles close to the floor. It seemed like a pelican in search of fish.

I was puzzled for a second; it was like something straight out of a horror movie. When I caught myself, I stood there almost paralyzed with fear. The hair on my arms stood upright, and then I felt my legs get cold. What was happening? I got a hold of myself and without realising it I ran towards the cashier to checkout to be out of that place. I thought I was hallucinating because of the past few stressful days, and my lack of sleep. It was just my body speaking to me I thought.

"I am open on register five", was the ditsy, cheery peach of a voice that came in over the PA system. The voice slightly chortled just before the announcement disengaged, 'tee hee hee' was the sound that escaped. I was already in line, but curiosity called out my name. I had to see this person, register five it was. I got there and it caught me by surprise when I saw it was not at all a girl and he was no Calista Flockhart either, he was built like Mike Tyson. I tried so hard to hold in the laughter; apparently I tried too hard because as soon as I walked up to the counter, I broke down into the loudest, giddiest laughter I had ever experienced.

After the whole ordeal I continued to check out trying my best to muster up all my composure not to laugh. It was impossible not laughing but I did my best. Suddenly the voice said to me, "Care to share the joke bud?"

I felt the laugh coming, it's a good thing he had already checked my groceries and supplies! I started to reply, my voice still shaky with the remnants of the joke, "Well, the thing is I remembered a good old joke and it kind of tickled me", trying to look away from his face, my eyes caught onto his neck where I spotted a tattoo that read *Mr.Bigs*.

I held it in till he was all done and I jolted out the double automatic doors which seemed to take forever to let me out. I ran to be clear of the store. I couldn't hold it in anymore. My eyes watered, my chest burned, the pain of suppressing the laughter was unlike any pain I had ever felt.

The uproar of laughter that escaped me was uncontrollable, I felt light headed. I walked over to my car in the rain; it was now more forceful than it had been when I first got there. It seemed darker and the wind was more gusty and violent and the faint trails of day seemed no more. I thought to myself, 'weather... such a strange thing'. I rushed to my car jumped in all wet and threw my bags onto the back seat. Started up my engine and headed home, on the drive I realised just how much it had rained, the storm drains were over flowing and on some streets the road was undetectable. Suddenly I remembered the tragic event that had taken place a few weeks earlier.

I got home and thought about the DNA test that I had done a few days earlier. Since Peter already knew the truth, it was time to let him know what I had done. I felt horrible for keeping it from him but because of the circumstances surrounding his situation I did not have much of a choice. Peter was no longer called Crazy Pete, though nobody knew about his daughter still being alive the situation was a bit tricky. I needed to know more about the curse. The more I thought about things, the more I thought that the footage of Anthony taking Serita and the phatom trying to get her a few hours later seemed weird. If he was working with them, it was odd that after viola had placed the phatom, he went ahead and took the child. He was up to something, and how is it the demon was unable to sense that he was there.

My phone rang while I was deliberating, it was Latricia. She asked me to come over because she needed to speak to me. I was nearby so I let her know I'd be there in a few. I got there and she was standing on the porch in a mini shorts and a vest, I parked in the drive way and she came to the car and sat down. She greeted me, giving me a kiss and hugging me. She got right to it.

"Shaun, I've been thinking about things lately and they've been bothering me. Like the accident, okay we figured that it was black magic and evil and all that, and some people are not so keen to believe such things. They go by what they can see, but there are a lot of things we don't see but we believe in them. Is it that we're just too blind or just too naïve to accept the truth for what it truly is?

"Like Peter's situation. Everyone was against him, treating him like nothing because he was labelled as crazy whether they knew his past or not, it never occurred to them that maybe his side should have been considered. Like just opening our minds or listening to him. If he were a famous person or a celebrity he'd just be considered as outlandish or eccentric. Yet, he knew he wasn't crazy or anything though he had some sketchy moments but nobody gave him the time of day. They all shun him. It was like a bible story."

She was right, how could someone forget someone who'd done so much for them? How could everything that had been done just be rendered as irrelevant. He had done so much for everyone, for the town, for the island. He gave selflessly to all. In his time of need he was treated as nothing. Nobody had remembered any of it. Some things only matter to people in their time of need and when the need has been met, nothing matters. They seem to forget; the selfish ways take over and out the door goes values and morality. Appreciation should be something that lasts a lifetime.

"Well, that's just how people are. There are some who are different but most people only look out for their own. It's not right but some people are prideful and they think of themselves as better than others until the moment comes where they need someone. When most people are in need, most of the things that they hold onto are released for that moment that they require the assistance of another. They let go of their prejudices, their narrow-minded ways, racism or beliefs.

"You ever notice that when someone needs an organ or blood they never ask who the donor is... All they care about is their life being saved then they're back to their old ways. Don't worry about it. Sometimes in life one voice might make a change, it takes one person to change a crowd, but most people are too afraid to follow what is right, they maybe fear being in the lower percentile. Most people go with the majority, going against what may be right All you can do is your best, we can't change people but we can start by being the different voice."

She seemed to be thinking for a moment, her eyes were blank. "You know what? I can understand that. I haven't known Mr. Alexandre long, but from what I've seen of him I see his humility. He has this meekness about him that no matter what he will help, and he doesn't ask for anything in return, he never mentions anything about it. He just does what he has to and that's the end of it. He doesn't ask for as much as a thank you. He is patient, kind and just good. I guess he is truly at that point in his life. The bible does say 'the meek shall inherit the earth' and that he is."

She had made valid points. "I think he has understood life I guess. I mean he was this super lawyer, the things he has seen. At such a young age he was so accomplished and then all the tragedy and to cope with everything... I don't quite understand it, but I guess that his demeanour helped him get this far and to come out of that whole mess." I didn't know exactly what I meant by that. "Now the only thing is his daughter. Do you think we should do anything in that situation?"

"That has been on my mind. I mean as a child of that age I think I'd want to know who my real parents were. I'm sure there are no childhood pictures with the Tates, and these people are supposed to be her parents. She may ask about her childhood. I am not saying anything bad about them but I am sure she has had questions. They also have no resemblance to her I mean there are a few slight things but nothing spectacular. Seeing the pictures of her, Peter and her mom, she looks like them."

"Maybe we should talk to Peter and see what he thinks. I mean it should be a lot easier now. He knows everything about himself so the memory curse is no more but the town's people still have not remembered everything including his daughter. I somehow think there's another curse in the workings... we need to find out."

"You know Shaun I called Linda and she said something about the curses. She said the memory charm was tampered with. Someone within Lilith's crew was doing things leaving loopholes and spaces, like not completing the curses. She thinks that one of Lilith's henchmen has turned against her and is working against her from within the group. Like a double agent kinda. The person must be really powerful, powerful enough for Lilith to not have noticed a thing."

"Interesting... I have been thinking why did the memory curse not fully work on Peter, and why did his memory only retain certain things."

"Maybe it was so Lilith would not notice that the curse was done wrong." I thought about it for a second.

"Latricia!" I exclaimed realising something. "Anthony Hank or Viola, I think we need to really get more of a background."

We agreed to follow up on that and speak with Peter and get his opinion on the matter. Father Monroe would also be a critical help to unravelling everything as he'd been more knowledgeable with most of these things. He'd be able to shed light on a lot. Linda Wright also in her books had provided tons of information that was very valuable. I was eager to finally get to meet her. Just a few more days to go but I was impatient.

I headed home. Every day there was something new or something that we had missed that started to make sense. I would be home for the next two days until the storm had cleared up. The weather was horrid. Lightning and thunder threatened above and the winds had gotten worse. The sea was washing up past the shore unto the roads. People were putting more sand bags as the water had started to climb over those that had previously been put up.

By the time the storm made landfall, it had become a hurricane. People's roofs, pieces of galvanise, pieces of wood, metal and other debris flew around threateningly. The power had gone out and transformers were being knocked down as well as utility poles, rendering most services inoperative. The phone lines were all out, and the emergency alarm system had been activated. We were in a state of emergency. We'd seen many other hurricanes over the years; the funny thing about it is they all had nice names. Who'd think of a name such as Camille, Floyd, Diane, or Betsy as something menacing or even intimidating?

From day to day we are faced with the unpredictable forces of nature. The uncontrollable dangers that lurk in the shadows, not synthetic or manmade, but the real life threatening dangers of an almost 'non-existent' force, the weather was always present. Many a time we ignore the ever changing and intimidating weather patterns that threaten the very existence of mankind. Most of the time we would experience sunny days and droughts, rainy days and storms. We rarely had earthquakes, and tornadoes were not native to our region. Thunderstorms were also a frequent occurrence, almost monthly and at times weekly or daily. On occasion, very rarely we had the occasional hailstorms. All these forces of nature and more, but none more frightening to us than hurricanes; due to our location we would seldom experience other weather patterns. We had minor tremors and mini earthquakes, never had tornados. Though we are prone to various other weather disturbances, the worst one that we are most likely to be faced with is a hurricane.

Throughout the years our island and surrounding region had been afflicted, tormented and victimized by this fearsome disaster. Like many in the past, this hurricane had managed to claim lives and property around the island and others in its trajectory according to radio broadcasts. Any island in its path had been terrorised. Though it was forecasted by meteorologists days or even months before it hit; they only announced it as a storm. This storm had quickly turned into a hurricane, Hurricane Tomas. The damage that it left in its wake was never predicted by anyone. Nature gives signs but never anything solid. Predictions of weather are always good but aren't always a good indication of what was really to come, it was a situation where people on our island were taught to expect the worst and pray for the best. Though we were never able to prevent disasters such as this, we always took certain steps and measures to ensure safety or at the least prevent the amount of loss that is retained year after year. Somehow all we did was still not enough.

Paradise: A Hidden Truth

Many people had chosen to ignore the warnings issued, they maybe believed that like many times before the weather report would have been inaccurate, or maybe they were just arrogant and believed they were immune to the hazards of the hurricane. More than eighty-five percent of the time we were prone to threatening blows and major destruction, this was one of those times. Hurricane Tomas had flaunted his power and had wreaked ultimate havoc on our settlements. Some of the strongest structures had been torn down. Many homes were lost as well as lives and reports of casualties started pouring in. There were also a few reports of people that had not been seen who were assumed as missing.

Chapter 12

The Mist

We spent days trying to rebuild our town. The hurricane had badly beaten us and almost taken all that we had. There was a strange mist that lingered above the island. Thick fog was everywhere, but Paradise Falls had it the worse. I had just helped out with the disaster committee and was on my way to meet with Father Monroe, Peter and Latricia. It was only two days since the hurricane and we had done a lot of work clearing the streets and restoring services and the utilities. There was still no running water as the rivers were all muddy, causing the reservoirs to have water that was brown and sandy. We were quickly rebuilding and the community had really come together as we always did.

On my way to meet with Peter and Father Monroe I stopped at Latricia's place. From there we headed down to Oak Town Deli to grab some coffee and doughnuts and croissants. I got to the church grounds and there were vehicles parked there. There were still people down at the infant school as it was being used as a shelter. We went straight to the presbytery where we met Father Monroe and Peter already waiting. They were happy for the hot refreshments and sweet treats and other pastries we brought.

We all went to the entertainment room where we got right down to it, refreshments in hand munching as we went along.

"The news has been showing phony images, as well as delivering false reports of the hurricane ravaging through the other islands. At first I thought that it could be true I mean why broadcast false reports. I mean a hurricane at that magnitude can be very treacherous but the way it went from a storm to a category four hurricane... with nature anything is possible but that was just odd, it was absolutely abnormal." Peter weighed in.

"When Peter came to me with that, I spoke to the heads and they confirmed indeed that it was confined only to our island, but it was worse in Paradise Falls. It was like something that was conjured, like more evil, more spells. A good bit of lives were lost and many people went missing. We took it that the dark ones were claiming mass lives and performing huge or heaped sacrifices to gain more power faster. We then were under the belief that they were planning something. They were up to something more, something more evil was coming our way. Never in our time have we heard of something like that. So whatever we're up against is nothing to be toyed with." Father Monroe let out.

"So the storm turned hurricane was conjured?" Latricia asked with a confused look.

"Basically, that's what happened. The circumstances surrounding it were too deliberate. There is no way a storm turns into a category four hurricane just by making landfall. Hurricanes thrive on water and the warmer the water the better the chance of the hurricane getting stronger, but over land and only Tesoro, particularly Paradise Falls... It's just odd." Father Monroe said.

"I thought that weather could not be controlled." Latricia added, alarm in her voice.

"We thought so too, but when dark magic is involved, spells and trickery... pure evil, the things they do have proved to be beyond belief." Father Monroe added staring out the window. For the first time he seemed like he had questions of his own, but he masked it well.

"Well if that's the case and they went through that and showed that they had the power to control the weather, maybe they're letting us know that they mean business. Maybe they know what we know or something." I suggested as I thought.

"True, and this weird mist or fog. It's been just lingering." Latricia spoke looking more puzzled. "I've been seeing like dark misty smoke like things following me. Almost human like the way they move, but it hovers and seems to fly."

"I've been seeing it as well. The day the storm was coming and I was getting supplies I saw it at the store... like it was following me." I remembered.

Just then the main door to the presbytery sounded. We all looked at the other, as if in wonder. Nobody ever came knocking; they'd either call or go to the church or even to the secretary. Father Monroe got up and walked out the room heading toward the front. We heard him walking away and stopping. We heard sounds as if he had opened the peephole. The door opened, we heard him speaking and another voice responded. Then the footsteps were heard coming back through the hall. Someone was walking with him. No voices were heard, just the footsteps then they stopped halfway through the hall. Father instructed the guest to wait right where they had stopped and he continued toward us. When he got to the room he had that expression on his face, he looked like he wasn't relaxed, and an uneasy expression he tried to hide.

"Are you okay Father?" I asked concerned.

"Yes... Yes I am... We have a," he paused like he was thinking, "a guest." He continued as if that was not quite the word he was looking for. "He said that he'd like to speak with us all. That he had some important information; stuff that we would be needing in order to help us understand what has been going on a bit more."

"Oh, who is it?" Peter asked.

"Yes, we've never had a guest." Latricia said looking excited and eager to meet the mysterious visitor.

I sat quietly, I knew Father Monroe well enough to know that look. I had seen it before.

"Well, I guess..." He said drearily. "Come in!" He called out to the person still waiting in the hallway.

We heard the footsteps continue. Careful sounding footsteps as if the person was a bit apprehensive, hesitant to come and join us. Father Monroe looked increasingly irritated, he seemed like he was confused and wondering what exactly was happening. The footsteps continued slowly, they sounded more calculated, more hesitant. The person was nearing the doorway to the entertainment room. The footsteps became more reluctant as if the person was having second thoughts. Then he appeared at the doorway.

"Him?!" We all exclaimed questioningly in unison.

"Let's not be that way. Don't be too quick or hasty to judge." Peter interjected.

"What is he doing here?" Latricia asked.

"Please, please, let's just think about this. If he has something to say, then allow him. Offer him that liberty and treat him how we would want to be treated. After all he is human." Peter said convincingly.

"I should not have come. I thought the church was a place of refuge of reprise. I know many people don't like me and a lot of you have the wrong conception of me, or maybe I give off the wrong impression. There are no excuses, but I must do what I must. I have a reason. I don't want to be known as the jerk but I have to, if she catches light that I am weak, then that will be it. I know a lot of you think I am evil and ruthless and responsible for a lot of the shortcomings suffered by many but I've really only been trying to protect you all from her power. I can do it better from the inside. She trusts me. I am here because I know that whatever I say on the church grounds cannot be intercepted. These grounds are consecrated and no evil thing can tread upon holy ground." Anthony Hank spoke almost believingly.

"How can we believe you? And who is this *she* you speak of? How do we know that you aren't playing some trick on us?"

"You don't have to believe me. In time you will find out who she is, give me the opportunity to speak, just hear me out. It's all I ask. I would not risk coming here." He said humbly, his voice was a lot different from the arrogant bellowing runt he usually sounded like. "I know I am considered as the enemy, but if you give me a chance then you might see it's not all black and white."

"You took his daughter, you ruined this man's life-" Latricia said as she was cut short by Anthony.

"If you hear me out you will understand."

"Give him a chance to speak..." Peter said sounding irritated at the thought of what was coming.

"Thank you." Anthony said, shaking his head at Peter, gesturing his gratefulness for the opportunity. "What people know of me is only the bad. No one knows my history, or my story. I am not going to tell you anything about my life story from my birth but I will give you a better understanding of me, of who Anthony Hank is. Please just bear with me as I speak. I'll be more than happy to answer any questions or even accept your comments or whatever. I am not here to change your mind or perception of who I am... I just want to tell my story." As he spoke he looked around at each of us.

We all agreed and like Peter had reminded us, we are all human. Good or bad we are all human, some of us are just different from others and we all have freewill. Having freewill was a good asset, but at times it seemed like it only served to make things worse. The decisions people made, the things that they would do were not always the best but that was the thing about having freewill.

"Many of you know me as a jerk, or consider me a bully and I don't blame you. That's what you see on the surface. My parents died at a very young age, I was left to be raised by my grandparents. Everything I know I learned from my grandparents. They believed in the power of nature, using the elements for good. They taught me that all things are connected and there were ways to harness all the different powers. They taught me how to cast charms and spells and of course any power could be used to do good as well as bad. I learned to use my powers to help people, learned the various techniques to heal people even talk to the dead.

"The more I grew the more I learned. My grandparents were poor, but we were happy. They loved me, they gave me everything and even though they struggled, they ensured that I had everything. I met a girl and she helped me to control my emotions. Her name was Christina. She became my closest friend. During my teenage years my powers had grown to the point where I'd just think something and I could make it happen. I started using my powers to get back at people who had done harm to me, who had threatened my parents. I made sure we were safe and always protected.

"I got Christina pregnant when we were both in the tenth grade. It created a problem for her. Her parents wanted her to get rid of it and live a 'happy life'; the school tried everything to get her kicked out. I had to do what I had to. Her parents eventually kicked her out and my grandparents took her in. I got a job as a mechanic and started working saving money for my child and for my girl. When the baby was born, I asked my parents if we could use the barn as our home. I'd worked on it for years and made it into a nice relaxing space. It had everything to raise a family and four bedrooms. They allowed me. They were supportive not that they condoned the underage pregnancy, but they welcomed the new life.

"We got married at the end of summer and Christina gave birth to our baby girl that fall, so we named her Autumn. She grew well and my parents loved her they helped us take care of her and raise her. She was two years old when I left high school. My grandparents let me know that they had been saving money to send me to college. I didn't want to let them but they insisted. I started college and everything was going smoothly.

"I went to a local school in town and took my courses there. A few months after I started school, a strange lady had come to our town. It was relatively small, smaller than Paradise so everyone knew everyone. She started coming around my parents' place. They didn't trust her but they were a nurturing loving people. In no time my dad fell terribly ill and we didn't understand it. Nothing we did helped. We turned to doctors who couldn't do anything for us. After taking him to numerous doctors, we took him to our type of doctors. We then learned what it was, but it was too late. Magic like that, we didn't have the resources to combat it. It was alien to us and it took too much time getting counter spells to help.

"I left school during that time, we needed the money. I sold my car I took a loan from my boss down at the shop. It was too late to help him, the magic that she had used was worse than anything we had seen. It was only after time my mom learned the lady's true identity, my mom gave me all her books and taught me everything, she taught me all the dark tricks, all the spells. Mummy made sure that I didn't let Lilith know about my gift or my powers. She put enchantments on me and protected me. Lilith killed my dad I could not do anything. A few months later my mom died too, it was Lilith again. She knew she was going. That witch killed both my parents. She killed all my parents.

"She approached me demanding that I sold my soul and become one of her slaves, her minions. She told me that I had to kill my family. I knew what she was capable of so I agreed to all that she said. I needed to sacrifice the souls at a specific location; I would be the only one there. I went through all the books mom had left me and I found ways around it. I put a charm on my wife and daughter and changed their identity; I sent them away where they would be safe and able to live normal lives. I had to put memory spells on them. It was my only way of protecting them. If my punishment was to live my life knowing that they didn't remember who I was, it was worth it. I still support them, I send them money but as a business.

"That night I sacrificed two sheep at the location; the devil didn't know the difference between an animal's soul or that of a human. I killed a cat for the sacrifice as my soul and returned to Lilith. My plan had worked. She said that her master, the devil had accepted the sacrifices and I was now one of hers. I went along with it. I couldn't not do it because she would find me out. With my soul intact I kept learning all there was from her. I learned new tricks and forms of magic. I grew a power that was greater than I had imagined. I had never killed anyone.

"Skipping ahead, she decided she needed to get a new body, the body she was using was getting feeble and weak and worn out. Her face started to show. A woman centuries old, who thrived on others, she lived on through others. She needed more lives, more souls and she'd learned of a Madame Lenoiré. Rich, sick, woman with a family of twins, a history of twins... and she was dying. Lilith knew of all of her family and knew that Madame

Lenoiré had not told anyone about her illness, except for her caretaker who swore to keep her secret.

"We got to Paradise and waited for Madame Lenoiré to return from Montreal, from Peter's wedding. As soon as she got back, Viola stepped in and used her voodoo dolls to kill the caretaker, then Lilith transcended them both into the residence where a frail Lenoiré lay helpless. She consumed Madame Lenoiré. Lenoiré being a woman of strong faith, Lilith could not get her soul so she captured her spirit. She also did not know that Madame Lenoiré had Father Monroe come and deliver her last rites, committing herself, her soul to God. After becoming Lenoiré, she started becoming weaker. The last rites ritual had worked against her. Viola changed into the caretaker and they both maintained these identities.

"From then they conjured this scheme to have Peter and his family move to Paradise, and they also made Marié and her family move. Marié's twins, Lilith wanted to harness their power. If she got twins she'd have no need to keep changing bodies or anything to stay young and alive. Harnessing the power of twins is her ultimate goal then she could be untouchable, unstoppable. She'd have powers beyond imagination. I tried casting spells and enchantments to protect them but they didn't work as well, but there was some other magic at work, pure magic almost like some divine magic. Lilith went to the highest ranking demons to ensure her plans worked.

"Lilith had Viola kill the original babysitter for the Thomas's. She took her form and learned the residence then return as herself later after Peter's wife had placed a request for another babysitter. Peter was away on a business trip, Viola returned to the house casting spells and curses all over. I was too late I couldn't do much to protect the family. I knew Lilith would personally attack Peter's wife Serena, so I did not enter her room. If I did she'd know that I was not loyal to her.

"Just before the phatom was due to collect Serita, I came in and took her. I cast more spells on the house to protect Peter. Viola had worked the memory curses, so I used a love charm along with a memory charm against hers. I knew it would work on Peter, so he'd remember what he needed. I had to go along with the rest of the plan but I always kept trying to leave small clues so the parts of Peter's memory that Viola's curse had wiped out could return.

"I took Serita to the Tate's home and cast spells so they would believe they had adopted her, I cast more spells so the whole town would know just that story, protecting her as well as protecting Peter, the Tates as well as the other inhabitants of Paradise.

"I led Peter to the river that night so he would know, I knew he would remember, and that he would do the right thing." He stopped talking and looked around. He was emotional. A weight had been lifted off his chest. We kept talking for a while about everything, sharing certain stories. He told me that Viola had been following me, the dark mist I had been seeing was her. He said that his was not black; it was a dark grey with sparks of white and that he'd prove to me that night. He told us to maintain our same demeanour with him in public and if he ever needed to meet with us he'd send a signal in the form of a blue flame, a blue flame that would possess the details of place and time for he could not speak in the open unless it was consecrated grounds.

   After we were done it was time to head home. I dropped off Latricia and remembered I needed some supplies so went to the store. I walked through the aisles looking for snacks as well as razors and some groceries that my mother had asked for. As I walked collecting my groceries, I noticed a dark grey mist with white streaks in it; it swooped around me and disappeared. I felt odd, but kind of relieved. Anthony Hank was really a good guy? His story left questions. It left us befuddled, questioning so many things. I headed back to my car and embarked on the half hour drive back home. I thought about it for a minute, but something came over the radio that caught my attention. 'A winter's day, in a deep and dark December. I am alone, gazing from my window to the streets below, a freshly fallen silent shroud of snow. I am a rock! I am an island!'

   Paul Simon and Art Garfunkel, musical geniuses, that was a song from my childhood days growing up. My aunts and mother always played the oldest music ever, at first I hated them. At that time these songs just sounded like pots and pans banging by delinquent children, I grew to love them. Another splendid hit played right after, 'I am the City' by ABBA.

   Right in the middle of my musical drawback, I heard that strange familiar sound again. Sirens and horns blaring, it seemed just too odd for this small town. I changed course and proceeded to the sounds of the sirens. The route was recognizable and I was wondering if my house was on fire. I drove even faster! Then I heard a siren coming from behind me, I checked my rear-view and noticed it was a police trooper.

"Shucks! Not now!" I was even more enraged. I slowed down and started to pull over. To my surprise he just sped right past me like he was on a mission. I thought that something really serious must have happened for him to pass me like I hadn't been breaking the law. I got back on the road and sped right behind him, being cautious enough to keep a safe distance, but I didn't have to for too long, he stopped right in front of my Cousin Beatrice's house.

On the driveway was a collage of emergency vehicles. Where once stood a beautiful house, were the charred memories of what used to be. I was flustered. I didn't know what to think. I rushed out of my car, and went straight up to the police barricade where I demanded to know what was happening. Even though it was obvious that there was a fire, but you never expect something like that to happen especially to your family. I pushed right through running up to what used to be the porch where Officer Andrew Johnson grabbed me like an untamed wildebeest. "I'm sorry Shaun, but you can't go in there" he said with the most sincere tone.

"What happened?!" tears rolled down my face as I spoke. "Are they okay?"

"Well, I am sorry to be the one to say this to you... I really wish I didn't have to be the bearer of bad news, but to put it plain and simple they're dead. We found only one body so far, it was Beatrice."

"Wh-- who? What? WHAT?!"

I completely lost it. I blacked out. A few moments later, I found myself sitting at the back of an ambulance. A nurse had me covered in a blanket type sheet, her nametag read: Cynthia White, she was standing in the doorway where I sat. Inside there was a male paramedic wearing white scrubs, his name was Marco Martinez.

"We've got contact" he shouted as my eyes slowly opened.

"Are you feeling okay Mr. Snow?" Cynthia asked in the most calming voice.

I nodded and looked around again, I saw Andrew standing next to one of the fire brigades that was parked on the lawn. I got up and headed straight towards him. He was busy talking to Jane Edwards the fire chief. He saw me coming and signalled her that he wanted to be excused. He walked towards me and the look he gave me let me know that I was out of control. Emotions had overwhelmed me. The reality of the day hit me like a bus. I dropped to my knees, uncontrollable tears and screams of anguish were all that managed to escape me.

As I lifted my head and looked over at what remained of Beatrice's house, I noticed a figure mysteriously floating away. Stunned, I stammered in shock, "L-l-l-o-, Look over there!" Pointing in the direction of where I had spotted the figure. It seemed to be standing in the middle of what used to be the hallway.

Marco and Cynthia both looked up, the expressions on their faces indicated that they too were confused as to what they were looking at. Immediately Andrew reached for his holster with his right hand, meanwhile holding the megaphone with his left.

"You there, halt!"

Almost at an instant the entire crowd responding to the emergency was facing that direction.

"Stop, or-or or I'll be... I'll shoot!" He said with fear in his voice.

Chief Wiggin Tubbs started to walk closer to the house, armed with his shotgun in his hand, closely behind him was Officer Andrew. Cynthia was standing there as if paralyzed, dread in her eyes as she stare in awe.

The hooded figure moved forward slowly towards the crowd. As it did, shots were fired from the policemen. It raised its arms or wings it resembled the grim reaper or a dark angel. As soon as it took the shape of a bird ready to take flight, all the gunfire ceased, the weapons were raised into the air, slowly turning to face their respectful owners. Hands were raised in surrender.

A bright light emerged from the figure almost blinding and then it was gone, only leaving behind a wisp of what appeared to be smoke. The guns all dropped to the ground. Chief Tubbs and his officers all raced to where the figure once stood-nothing. At least nothing that would've been spotted at first glance.

I rushed up to the others, the questions in my head fluttered around. Nothing made sense. A hooded figure, no visible face, it seemed to just be dark matter with a cloak on. It was supernatural. What was really happening in our small town of Paradise Falls?

*　　　*　　　*

Paradise: A Hidden Truth

When I got home it was three in the morning. A terrifying chill lingered in the air. My mind raced from the events of the days past. What was becoming of our town, our peaceful incident free town? I stayed up going over everything. I was so jazzed on coffee; there was no way I was sleeping. Reliving the loss, pain and hurt, just anguish- it left a dark cloud, my emotions were stirred, my heart felt dead. I needed to know what was happening in Paradise. I felt like Beatrice's death was my fault, like it was a warning. The thing looked directly at me. As it if was ensuring that I knew I was noticed. What was it about me that they were after? Or were they even after me at all. The things I had been seeing. I started to think of them, I remembered little things.

I had to let mom know that Cousin Beatrice had passed without rising too much of an alarm. Cousin B had been my care taker and babysitter, she was not a blood relative but due to how close she was to my family we saw her as family. Abandoned by her own parents as a child, she was taken in and was raised by my grandparents with my mom and the other siblings. She was always pleasant, she just took care of her children as her husband had been working a lot. She was a teacher but got time off, maternity leave. They only found one body from the fire. As I thought about it, alarms went off in my head. They only found one body but she had three children. She had my godson and the twins... The Twins! I remembered what Anthony had told us about twins. She had been attacked just to get her children. What had taken place? Who did the remains at the scene belong to? Where were the others?

Chapter 13

Meeting Linda

I had to speak with Anthony Hank, I needed questions answered. He was close enough to Lilith to shed light on what was happening. Speaking with him was my best bet. I didn't know if I could trust him but my instincts gave me hope that I could. I trusted my instincts as they had never failed me. Instincts were God's way of protecting us, of showing us something that we had missed, delivering a message that we had neglected, a gentle reassurance that He was watching over us. I couldn't speak Anthony had warned that anything spoken on unholy ground would be heard by Lilith. He said she had many slaves or minions all over and if we paid close attention, we'd know who they were.

He was no longer a member of the board; the only way of getting to speak to him was by visiting his office. I thought about it for a while. The more I thought about him, I started to feel him, see his thoughts. My mind called out his name, and I heard his voice answer. I felt strange; I thought I was really starting to go crazy. He mentioned my name, it sounded like he was as puzzled as me, he questioned if it was me. I answered confirming my identity. He started to speak excitedly, he revealed that no one had ever spoken to him that way before, he started asking questions. He asked if I was an aura. I answered no; I didn't even know what that meant.

I told him that I needed to meet with him; I had more questions especially since the incident at Cousin Beatrice. He laughed and answered, we have no reason to meet... we can discus it here, in privacy. In here you can tell if I am lying, in here you can read my mind. Unless you haven't unlocked your powers completely... I questioned the powers thing, I questioned if this was even real or happening. He answered, and said it was real as everything else that had been happening. He then asked if that was an inside thought or a question for him. I answered that it was an inside thought. Was I really going crazy? I had reached that point, or was I going through an early midlife crisis?

Anthony's let out a thunderous laugh. Oh man, he was hearing me! I needed to be careful what I said... I mean what I thought. He suggested that I try to differentiate messages from thoughts. He added that it was just like having a normal conversation, just a more private one. He asked what I wanted to talk about. I told him about the day after he spoke with us at the presbytery, I wanted to know what happened at the store and for sure it was him. He described everything in great detail. I was building my trust for him, it happened almost automatically. I asked why he had saved Serita, why he had gone through all the trouble of helping her, why he cast the counter curse to help Peter remember, and why he hadn't cast one on Serita so she could also remember.

He explained that it would be more difficult to cast a spell like that on her because of her tender age, he explained the repercussions it could have had and how it could have affected her negatively. He also said that if he did, she would have most probably been killed as soon as Lilith found out and the Tates as well as Peter would have been killed. He wasn't fearful of losing his life but he wanted to protect them. He explained that he didn't want Peter to lose all he had, all he had worked for and he didn't want him to go on living as he himself had. His wife and daughter were still alive and he'd maybe never get a chance to show them who he was. He made sure that Peter always had the memory of his daughter, and that one day Peter and his daughter would be reunited, that she would know her real father. I was seeing Hank in a new light. The tough front was only to keep up his reputation with Lilith, so she'd never question his loyalty to her.

I grew a soft spot for Anthony Hank, I respected him and as a man I saw it fit to apologise for our incident... our first run in. He said it was no problem. He said that it made it easier to get things done, and to snoop around without Viola or Lilith or any of her underlings suspecting anything. He laughed it up a bit, he enjoyed the rush and the entertainment, and he also wondered how I knew so much about him. I thought about it for a while and I couldn't find any explanation. It was like things had just come to me, I was seeing parts of his life as I got angry. He told me I'd learn more from Linda. I wondered how he knew about that. He explained to me that I had powers, but he didn't know much about them. He had sensed something in me, something hidden but he hid it from his mind as he didn't want to let it off, didn't want the wrong people knowing about it, because they would be after me. Little did he know, there were already things after me, for years since my memory had served me, there were things after me.

While thinking of the creatures I had seen, I saw images of them flash. Anthony had seen them as I saw them... he knew most of them except for the darkest one, the demon of death. I felt his emotions... his heart was racing. He was scared. He asked how I had survived any encounters with it. His fear was growing alarmingly, I tried to calm him. Confused, lost I began praying the twenty third psalm. As I prayed, the words became gibberish... I was forgetting the words. Something else was there, a woman dressed in white but there was something dark; I tried to focus but whatever it was fully intended on ensuring the words were alien to me.

The woman in white faced the creature, she was fearless... She seemed to be protecting us, fighting the demon off. Then Hank continued, he was praying along with me. Conviction in his voice, his voice was stern as he said the words with valour. I felt myself getting stronger, my confidence was boosted. I said the words along with him, focusing and meditating on them. I started saying them out loud. The words took effect and we had managed to ward the demon off. The woman in white grabbed both of us and ascended. Slowly smoke had surrounded the creature and started receding. I found myself lying on the floor of my bedroom, cold sweat. Short of breath and breathing deeply, I wondered what just happened.

I got up and staggered across the floor entering the hallway toward the bathroom, I felt weak, as if I had been bludgeoned. I headed to the sink and started washing my face generously with cold water. I tried to slow down my breathing. I heard the front door open and close and mum's voice asking if I was alright. I convinced her that I was okay that I only had a bad dream. I started to feel better; gradually my breathing had slowed down, returning to normal. I questioned my experience, whether I was dreaming or having a nightmare, what the creature was doing in my dream wondered why I felt so cold... Anthony Hank! He was there and we were speaking... it wasn't a dream. The lady in white, she looked angelic, a soothing glow. White and golden radiant beams of light emerged from her, her aurora was calming... comforting.

Trying to get my thoughts together, I realised if this truly happened, I never got a chance to ask what I really wanted to. I knew that one of Viola's servants was responsible for whatever happened to Beatrice and her family but it wasn't Hank. I needed to know what he knew about it. I was prepared to fight, exact my revenge on them. I called Father Monroe, I needed to tell him what had just happened... the conversation, the creature, the woman in white... She had rescued us, I felt different. He asked me to come down as soon as possible and I'd give him the details.

I took a quick shower, got dressed and hurried down to the presbytery where Father Monroe stood waiting at the entrance. We went inside and I immediately started speaking, almost unintelligibly. Father ushered me to a seat and asked me to slow down and relate everything to him. As I begun, I noticed his facial expressions. He looked stunned like he was impressed. He smiled in admiration as I retold the episode. When I got to the part about the woman in white, he went pale, he was astounded, elation. When I was done he showed me a book and asked me to look through it and point her out. When I started browsing through, I came across an exact match. The lady I had seen was the same woman on the book. She had thick long black hair, a small mole more like a beauty mark on her right cheek, captivating eyes and a perfect smile dressed all in white. The name on her picture was Emila; the book seemed to be written in Latin, a language that was alien to me.

There was a knock at the door, Father Monroe went to answer and came in with Hank. Hank stood looking dumbfounded, and then he came to me staring intently at me. He pointed at the book speechlessly, looking at the picture confound.

"Her, she was there! Emila Milagros! I've read about her, I've even heard the stories... but never did I imagine that I'd ever see her. She saved us, had it not been for her we'd be trapped in a coma-like state, spirits suspended between our world and theirs, we'd be in purgatory."

"Who exactly is she?"

"She is one of the defenders of the light, a warrior, a protector of life." Hank responded.

"A defender of the light? A protector of life? What is all of this?"

"Shaun you called upon her, she came to your rescue. You unlocked your telepathy, more will be unlocked... more will be awaken as time goes by." Father Monroe said with just in his voice. "You are special. You know your history, all of these things are not coincidental... there is still a lot more to you that you will learn as time goes on. We are in the middle of a battle between good and evil and many will perish. You were chosen, you were sent, handpicked by the Redeemer Himself."

"What exactly am I?"

"You are one, one of the light." Father Monroe answered.

Things had just been unfolding, everyday there was something new. I had no idea what he was speaking about. That was not what I came here for; I really wanted to know about Beatrice, what happened to her. I needed to know all that Hank knew.

"Hank, do you know anything about what happened yesterday? What happened to Beatrice?" I asked.

"Yes, I do... don't worry. She is okay, right now is not the best time. Lilith sent Andrew and Viola to burn the house down and reclaim the souls. She needs thirteen souls to awake some ancient evil. She managed to get seven during the hurricane. She needed the twins, Beatrice's kids. She couldn't get any souls from the accident; she couldn't use the spirits either. She decided to go after those near and dear to you. She targeted you. I knew they were going to attack so I sent Beatrice and the children away to a safe place. I left the bones at the house, I knew it was going to be burnt down and attacked. I went in there and sent them away." Hank had revealed.

"Shaun, don't you worry... they are safe where they are." Father Monroe added. He knew about it. "We didn't tell you because we had to make sure that our plan would be sound and maybe if you found out that her life was in trouble you'd have taken a different approach."

I was relieved, I wanted to know where they were... but I trusted that they were okay. We continued speaking about the event, about how strange everything was. Hank wondered how we survived the demon creature. It was his first time seeing it in real life. He'd only ever seen it in books that he read or stories that he had heard. As I sat I remembered that Jimmy was flying in today. There was so much going on. I knew with him being here I would have a piece of mind. Latricia and I had become a lot closer but the bond that I had with Jimmy was like no other. I let them know that I had to leave. I was thankful for all they had told me, though it wasn't much, it was all I needed to know. I greeted them and headed off to the airport to get Jimmy.

When I got to the airport his flight was just coming in. I was nervous and excited. I parked my car in the lot adjacent to the terminal and walked over. The airport was relatively small; the walk from the parking lot took one minute. The passengers started exiting the customs and immigration area into the arrivals hall. I run over to the waiting area where I stood eagerly gazing at the swinging doors as passenger after passenger exited. I finally saw him, I hurried over to him. I had anticipated this moment for the longest while.

"Hey! The Shaun man!" He hailed as he walked over. We shook hands and hugged each other.

"Jimmy! How was the flight down?"

"Long and tiring, do you know that there were no televisions or any entertainment on any of the planes smaller than the 767? The ticket cost an arm and a leg and all I got was six peanuts and a bag of air."

Paradise: A Hidden Truth

I laughed; Jimmy was just like his dad. He was right though, and made a valid point. No entertainment and nothing worth bragging about. We headed to the car and headed home. While driving we came across Ming's Palace, a local Chinese restaurant. It had been our favourite place to get food, and Jimmy was hungry. He'd left home at 5:00 a.m. It was 4:43 p.m. We sat down and had our meals. Catching up on everything, I couldn't speak openly about everything as I had been warned that it was not safe, but everything else that was already spoken about publicly I filled him in. I also tried the telepathy thing on him. It didn't seem to work. Maybe we were both too tired. We drove home where mum had prepared a meal. There was nothing better than a home cooked meal. After eating we went to the game room where we both fell asleep.

The next morning I woke up not realising I had fallen asleep. Jimmy was still fast asleep, worn out and tired. I left him my other phone and a note letting him know I would be out for a while. That day I headed down to the station. As I got there, I met Linda Wright a fifty four year old woman with a heavy French accent. A woman of class, she was petite and didn't look a day over thirty. She was one of the original descendants of the people who once made the community what it was; she was a distant relative of Madame Lenoiré. She was never out much and lived far off on the outskirt of the Village of Paradise Falls. A quiet woman, a slender figure, she was affluent and she had earned her wealth earnestly and honestly, she had been the head doctor at the Paradise Falls Hospital. As rumour would have it, she was originally from Lyon, France.

She never spoke of her past either, but I'm sure if asked by the right person in an appropriate manner, she would.

"Good Morning Miss Wright" I said with obvious elation in my voice.

"Good Morning Mr. Snow, How are you doing today?"

She knows my name! She knows my name! I could swear I heard my mind crying out loud as I thought 'she knows my name!'

"I am doing great Miss Wright, well besides all the tragedy you know. I mean it's an honour to meet you!"

"Well if I may, the pleasure is all mine. Actually, you're the reason I am here."

At this, I was stunned I didn't know what to expect. The look on her face had suddenly gone frigid, as if telling me whatever it was had been urgent.

"Shaun, please just-"

Before she could finish, Officer Andrew interrupted almost out of nowhere, "*Linda*, I see you're out visiting our fine citizens, blessing and gracing us with your presence. To what do we owe the pleasure of your visit?" a tone of obvious sarcasm in his voice.

"Well Andrew if you must know, I am actually here to see Mr. Shaun Snow. Have I been in violation of any real crimes? Maybe there's too much work to be done that you'd just prefer be a nuisance to senior citizens?"

"I actually find it rather enticing giving a hand out to those who really need it; I figured you're a ways from home and might be lost?"

"If I were lost, I trust that you'd be the right person to come to right? By the way Andy, you might want to fix your undershirt, your tag is showing."

"Um... right, I guess we'd get out of your hair now Andy, we'll just be on our way" I interjected.

We proceeded to walk away, with Miss Wright leading the way, as I looked back I saw Andy standing there highly livid, he was red with fury. Linda took hold of my arm and dragged me away, almost as if beckoning a child.

"Avoid his stare Shaun. Let's get to my car. We need to leave the town for a while. Don't ask any questions."

With that, I just stay shut and followed her to her car. We got to the back parking lot and I reached for the door to a 2005 Toyota Prius. The door opened and I sat in the passenger's side. I looked over and saw Linda just standing there looking at me with a straight face. Her hand held the door to a black Ford Mustang with silver trimmings and not just any ford Mustang, but the new 2010 GT Premium two door Coupe.

"Wrong car," she said with a glimmer of a smile, with this she looked over to the driver's side of the Prius "Mr. Tubbs, how are you today?"

I was in complete disbelief, talk about a kick in the teeth. Looking over I could see Chief Tubbs standing there like a gargoyle, I could tell by his look that he was not at all pleased, but then I thought 'when is Chief Tubbs ever pleased?'

I mustered what little regard I had for myself and quickly ejected myself from his car. I started to laugh inside and sauntered over to Linda's car, never looking back at the huge mass of nothingness that stood next to the Prius. Linda and I got into the car.

"Really Shaun? A Prius? I would not be caught dead, face down at the bottom of a lake in one of those things. I am a woman!" she had the brightest smile on her face, and started to laugh!

"Well..." I paused for a second to think of something I could say that would not sound completely naive and ridiculous. I realised there was nothing, "it's quite a piece of heavy artillery you have there. I drive a Rav 4." I got a laugh out of her with that.

"Here, check out what this baby can do!" she exclaimed with a twinkle in her eye. I felt my body thrust back into my seat a she geared the little black Mustang zero to sixty in just fewer than six seconds. I was amazed at this dare devil just relaxed in her little cockpit, the look on her face so jovial and youthful! "Whoooooooooooo!" she exclaimed as she reached speeds of over ninety miles per hour.

We had great roads, great roads that began wrapping around hills and slopes. There was only one road in to our town and one road out, and we were on that road leaving. We approached the Vérité Bridge. Over the radio I could hear Tracy Chapman pouring her heart out performing 'Crossroads'.

I swayed to the music as we crossed the bridge, absorbing the soulful melody. Linda began speaking as we came up on the halfway mark, "Enjoying the drive?"

"I am, quite relaxing and find this interesting. Why do we not have a nature magazine?"

I realised that I hadn't been to this side of town in years. I looked around and the splendour of the scenery had me paralyzed. The wide river so far below, but you could hear the gentle flow as it carried its course, tilting and winding below-tripping over rocks and tiny pebbles.

"It could be that most are too preoccupied or maybe the fact that no one really ever pays attention to the little things in life." She responded.

Just as I was about to answer, I looked over at her. What I saw had me completely awestruck.

"It's in bad taste to stare at a lady Mr. Snow" her voice sounded different. "Don't say anything just yet."

We got to the other side of the bridge where a sign welcomed us to Pike Creek, a quaint town, even smaller than Paradise. I never had the opportunity to take in the sites and all the things that this town had to offer. It was the town that time never touched. Historic buildings everywhere, cobblestone roads, small stone paths and even at some point the occasional dirt road, very carefully crafted. Nothing was different about this town from the day it was built. After turning unto a winding dirt road, we came upon a well preserved picturesque shingle home. Its carpentry was splendid. I'd had never seen anything quite like it, well only in the movies.

Chapter 14

Truth and Consequences

"I'm bringing you here so you can learn something. I know you love history, so hopefully this little lesson will interest you. I know what you just saw is all a bit puzzling for you, maybe a bit much for you to understand, but in life not everything is as it seems. This town of Pike Creek is really called Truth and consequences. To those who know, we know. The name Pike Creek is only a friendly moniker, like the bright neon lights to a restaurant. It was called this in hopes of hiding and banishing a dark history.

"I will tell you a little bit about myself, it might be a little much to take in all at once but believe me. My real name is Edvina Milagros; Linda Wright is the name I use to hide my identity. I am a twin and believe it or not I am centuries old.

"What you just saw, the change you noticed, happened because spells and enchantments don't have the same effect as they would especially around evil. This town is sacred. No evil dwells here, they can't be here for too long either. So I transformed to my real self. There is no need for me to keep my identity hidden here unless my prism or my pendant alerts me.

"This town is protected by ancient spells, protected from demons of the darkness and from reapers. Some things are easier to understand if they are seen, just as the bible says 'deliverance from the snare of the fowler and from the noisome pestilence'.

"These evil beings, they can't stay hidden out here after about forty five minutes or less they take their true form, any evil charms or spells fail. Light is all that is needed for one's true identity to be revealed.

"Many people don't believe in anything that they cannot see, or anything that seems out of the ordinary, but the truth is, not because it isn't seen or known to you, that doesn't mean that it doesn't exist or that it is not there.

"In Paradise or anywhere outside of Consequences, one must be careful of what he or she says, 'for once it reaches the air, it reaches evil's ear'. The things that speak the loudest are those that bear no sound. The loudest sound anyone can hear is silence.

"You will learn a great deal here Shaun, even about yourself. Please keep an open mind, I know some of what you have seen and it will be explained here as well."

Miss Linda had thrown a hardball right at me. I never expected any of what she had said. Questions were flowing through my head, memories of that creature, the people that I saw that no one else did and the sounds I heard that were mute to others. Images of this Lilith woman were filling my head. This journey, my life had been a long winding road and it became more complicated as I grew older. She went into detail about the things I had seen, she knew more about me than I had shared. I was puzzled.

"Miss Linda... I mean Miss Edvina" I didn't know what to call her, "What is all of this? How do you know about my past? How did you know about that- that creature?"

"It's a demon of death, not to be mistaken with what we know as the Grimm Reaper, but something even more maniacal, something worse, something more... dark. Abaddon or Sammael is his name. He is only seen by detentoribus lucis higher than the Bringers of Light, more specifically meaning, holders of the light, which you are. Your type is rare, only few holders of the light have been known and your story is the rarest yet. We, the bringers of light have followed you from the day of conception; we are your worldly protectors."

"Worldly protectors? Am I some sort of anointed disciple or something?" I asked jokingly.

"Basically, that's what you are... well not exactly. I don't know how to say this so I will just say it. You are an angel, sent to earth as a human to help with the battle between the light and the darkness. My brother can better explain it to you. Nathaniel knows more and understands a lot more than I do. He is one of us; he is also a healer and a revealer for lack of a better word. I cast spells and create new potions and ways of doing 'magic' without using elaborate words. Magic at one time required verbal spells, now we do a lot more from the mind."

"I am an angel..? Right, right... An angel who has lived an absolutely normal life? Struggles like all others? Suffering?"

"Yes, and you've also helped others. Remember you were sent here to live life as a human, so you're not immune to all things that 'regular people' go through. The things that you have seen and experienced, the things you have heard when all others heard silence. It's not a sign of insanity, but a sign of divinity. You feel sorry for anyone who is in a less than fortunate situation that they were not responsible for. How do you explain knowing a person's exact thoughts without being told them?"

"This is all so much; I mean I took most of this as a joke: like someone had been playing pranks on me."

"It's all real, every bit of it is real as you and me sitting right here today."

"So who is this Lilith woman? What does she want with these people? With the twins?"

"Lilith..." She said as if pondering, almost as if she was questioning. Her expression had changed. "Lilith, that witch, that vile, crude, disgusting creature. I know exactly who she is. She is... it is as old as time... Lilith is the devil's wife."

"The devil's wife?" I repeated, confused.

"Yes, the devil's wife. Lilith was the first woman to make a deal with the devil, she sold her soul. Her pain had made her evil. Her soul was blackened before she sold her soul. Her heart was just as putrid."

"I don't mean to sound stupid, but how is she or it the devil's wife." I asked even more puzzled.

"Well, you do know that evil has been around since good has existed. Some people thought of God and the devil as being one and the same, others believe that God and the devil are working hand in hand, some believe that God is the bad one while the devil, or Satan is good. Lilith happened to be one of those who believed that the devil was superior and better. She lost her family and went through tough times; she felt that God had failed her so she turned to the devil.

"She made herself available to him, she disowned God. She began worshipping and giving praise to Satan. She vowed to wreak havoc on those responsible for her pain. She went after their families, their friends. Satan realised her devotion to him, her readiness to serve him. He began testing her, giving her tasks to perform, causing confusion, putting nations at odds with each other. She created confusion all over, she quickly moved up the ranks. He gave her the option to become one of the demons, or to become his wife and live forever, where she would gain all the things she wanted, all she had to do was offer him great sacrifices and bear gifts.

"She took the more appealing one... she didn't want to be dead. She had no soul and thought that by becoming a demon she'd be a lowly unworthy slave. Always wanting to be in control she viewed this as a demotion, an insult to all she had done. So she took the offer and married him. She became untouchable and invincible... well almost. God sent his army of angels, or 'Those of the Light'. He could have easily ended that reign of evil and terror, but he is fair he made sure that he sent his army as normal humans to start from scratch and grow and become warriors of the light.

"Over the years, we harnessed the power of the light. We became wiser; we learned and improved our skills. We never killed; we would send our foes to a certain purgatory. We were made to protect humanity and to teach the ways of the light to those who were sent to us. Many of us died as expected in any battle, but a war is only a war when both sides are almost equally matched. Then the battle had become more enraged, more intense. They started going for certain people, people who possessed certain powers or gifts, people who had psychic abilities or other powers like telepathy or telekinesis and twins especially identical twins. Then they learned of your type, detentoribus lucis, who posed a threat from conception.

"Uneasily harmed and protected by portarent lucis. I've heard of your type, you're legendary but I've never seen one. Your birth holds many answers. As time passes on you will learn your powers, your powers are a lot greater than anyone could imagine."

"So I was destined to be a part of this?"

"Yes, you were sent here for this purpose."

"What about Anthony Hank? What is he?" I asked as I remembered his story.

"A remarkable man... One of the only regular humans I know who has become an aura because of his heart, his grandparents and his own training. What he is doing is risky, but honourable. No one had dared to do what he is. The way he stands by her, learning all her ways and trying to prevent her powers from harming others. I just fear for his life."

"Wow, so he was telling the truth... Bianca... Peter Thomas. He appeared to me the other night."

"Yes, he is trustworthy. His deceiving Lilith is still remarkable. He is a wise one. Your cousin... James... He also is an aura. He sees things too. That's why he believes your stories." She had dropped another bomb on me.

"Jimmy, is an aura? Jimmy sees things? I mean he did mention he sees things but he never really went into detail."

"Remember when your grandfather died, you two saw the butterfly leaving the room and nobody else did?"

"How did you know about the butterfly?"

"Your grandfather was a lumen."

"So can I still have like normal human things, like date or go partying? Can I have sex? A normal relationship?" I asked naïvely.

"You can do all of them, you have freewill... the thing is you haven't because you have values and thanks to your upbringing, you respect others. I know you're a virgin, and not because you can't have sex... you've just turned down the offers you've had because you want something meaningful, a bond you can hold unto." She spoke like she knew all my details.

"Um... you know that I'm a vir- um a vir-vir-virgin..?"

"Shaun, I think you should just stop talking now and let's just walk to the house. All your questions will be answered, I assure you. Let me show you something first." She touched my temple and I felt a surge. I was her.

I felt myself getting more distant, I was still me but in her body. Going back in time, seeing things, hearing things. Things that had happened, things she had experienced... I was experiencing them. I saw an old house, a log house tucked away in the woods. I didn't recognise the place. There was snow, it felt cold. I looked and saw a woman, a good-looking woman dressed in white, dark black hair curly. Her clothes were odd, her hairstyle. She looked like someone from the historic European paintings. She was absolutely beautiful. She looked like the woman from the book, the woman from Hank and my encounter. I was a baby, a little girl. I looked over in the crib next to me and there was a little boy.

The beautiful woman spoke to us in a foreign language, a language that I understood. She was hiding us under a bed. She called us her darlings, her children... her twins. Silence had filled the cabin, I peeked from under the bed and I saw a dark figure. Our mother had a silver cross clenched in her hand and was engaging in battle with the figure. It had attacked dispersing black flaming dragons. They were both speaking... a foreign language. The dark figure, a reaper had asked her to give us to it. She refused, waved her hands and said some words in Latin, Lumen ad draconum! Evanescant extemplo! Light to the dragons, vanish at once; it was an incantation, a spell. I seemed to understand everything that they were saying. I felt frightened. The dragons disappeared, leaving smoke in their wake. She spoke directly to the reaper, addressing it by name, Glatisvar. His feet hadn't touched the ground; he was floating almost ghostlike in mid-air. White sparks of light exuded from the spot where Glatisvar was, leaving behind a coin. I noticed the same coin from the evidence collected at the accident.

She bundled us into a carrier shot out lightning like lights, placing us securely onto her as she ventured deep into the woods. I woke up to a voice along with Emila's, our mother; mum had referred to her as Samira. A woman with whitish crystal like eyes, silver and diamond hair that looked like it was flowing in the absent wind, Her skin was translucent, she was shiny, almost looked like a pearl. We were in a castle of some sort, there was light everywhere. It resembled an ice castle, but it was made of all white and clear gems, minerals and crystals. Samira had rescued us. The images were cut short, Linda had let go of my temple. I felt stronger, I felt something inside... something inexplicable.

Chapter 15

The Experience

Standing on the veranda stood a tall slender man, he appeared to be in his early forties. He stared intently at the vehicle. A lady sat in a rocker under a mini arch in the corner; she didn't seem to have noticed us. She just gazed blankly into the fields. We walked up to the house and the thoughts and visions of all I'd seen and experienced rushed through my head.

"Nathaniel! How are you doing?" Linda called out.

Not too bad Miss Linda, we've certainly missed you around these here parts", he returned with somewhat of an accent.

"Oh Ataiel, you know I was only here two days ago", she replied with a mini chuckle, her face now turning blush.

"That's to show ya, we miss yuh bad when yuh gone!" He turned his focus to me, "and who is this strapping young lad you brung wit ya?"

"This here is Shaun Snow. Shaun just moved back to Paradise from Maine. He spent a few years studying and working."

With that he looked directly into my eyes, his expression changed. An expression of grim had appeared, he hid it well but he was obviously uneasy.

"Good day Mr. Nathaniel," I uttered hand outstretched. "It's a great and sincere pleasure to meet you."

A smile spread across his face, revealing the most perfect teeth I had ever seen. "This here is Edith, she don't talk much... in fact... she don't talk any. Not since..." He went quiet. "Where are my manners?" he asked stretching out his hand.

He reached for my hand and gripped with the firmest clutch. His eyes went grey, I felt my thoughts rushing. I felt my heart singe, irregular beats then I saw darkness all around me. I felt liquid; I couldn't smell anything all I could see was black. I was submerged in something, I tried to look at my hand but all I could make out was a blur. Raising it closer to my face, I could make out a baby's hand. My hand. I felt my head, almost hairless. Where am I? Who am I? What is happening?

I couldn't grasp what was happening. I felt my body going down towards my belly, I felt something long and slimy. It was an umbilical cord; I was in my mother's womb. I could hear faint muffled sounds, one sound in particular stuck with me; it was a female voice. The familiar sound so soothing, it was my mother's voice, young and strained. I could not make out what she was saying, but the pleasant tone seemed ecstatic.

"Mrs. Snow, I fear that you have fibroids and need to undergo surgery as soon as possible." I heard a male voice saying.

"I do not have fibroids Dr. Harris, I am telling you- I am pregnant! I know that I am, I am not asking you, and I will not be doing any surgeries either! You know what?! I'll see myself out! Thanks for nothing!" I had never heard my mother this enraged.

I felt a hard thud, as if someone had hit her belly. I felt a rush; her blood seemed to get warmer. I knew that feeling ever too well, after all I felt it many times myself.

"Why don't you watch what you are doing? You jack ass! Did you not see me coming? You deliberately tried to run me over? You brainless dim-witted fool! If I miscarried it would be your neck on my silver platter! You insolent idiot!" Mummy was clearly having a moment. I was really enjoying the show, though I could not see what was happening.

"I apologize ma'am" I heard a male voice say, with no sincerity in his voice, "I never even saw you coming; I don't even know how I swerved into you."

"Exactly, you swerved into me, how could you have missed me? You were looking directly at me! I am pretty hard to miss at this stage."

'Get him mummy!' I thought to myself as I listened in to the commotion. Changes again, more changes; I was now able to see not only inside the womb, but outside of it. People were all around I recognised a few faces, faces that I had seen before also strange faces, not only faces but strange creatures. They were all over. I noticed that thing that had been haunting me, the dark creature. I saw Edvina, and Nathaniel. They were in public places following my mother, fighting off creatures as they went along. All Edvina had told me was true. I was seeing things for myself.

An elderly woman, following my mother in the shadows dressed all in black. She was now at the grocery store; she came to my mother and started a conversation. She lurched forward secretly, attempting to strike my mother's womb with a concealed gold dagger that came from her finger like a nail. 'Don't talk to her' I thought, raising my hand in defence 'she's evil.' I saw Nate and Linda coming toward my mother; she didn't seem to notice them. The woman on the porch came into view, just as the elderly woman in black reached to touch my mother's belly, the lady from the porch struck her hand with a cane.

All of this was becoming even more frightening. I started to see through the eyes of others, feel what people felt, know their thoughts. I could see peoples' spirits, their souls and in those who had no soul, I saw dark entities. I saw demons; people dressed in transparent black cloaks, almost invisible, there were those in white cloaks as well, not visible to other mortal beings or regular humans.

A familiar voice swept upon my audible range, a voice I did not like; we were at the hospital again, my parents and I. A lab tech was coming toward us wheeling a gurney as we sat in the waiting area. His eye fixated on my mother, on me. As he spoke I recognised he was the same one who ran into her the last time she came for a check-up. He was after us again. Nathaniel was right behind him, walking calmly and slowly. He winked at me a smile spread across his face, and he directed my vision at the male lab technician, he had used a petrifaction spell on him. A wave of his hand and the stone figure disappeared. It seem like he had paused time, no one seemed to notice what was happening.

"Mrs. Lauren Snow? The doctor will see you now, room eleven." A female voice announced over the P.A. system.

My father got up and held my mother as they walked through the hall over to room eleven it was marked with black numbers above the door. Bursting open as we were led through by a female doctor were the double doors with frosted glass, bearing the words 'Maternity Ward' and just below 'Deliveries' in small print black writing. They helped mother into a hospital gown and assisted her unto the bed. The doctor who was supposed to perform the delivery walked in. She was pretty, flowing golden hair wrapped up nicely in tight curls. Her lips were red and her face was powdered. I looked at her, focusing on every detail, she started changing her face. It was Viola!

I felt angry, that evil heartless witch was in my delivery room pretending to be a midwife. Fists clenched in rage as I stare at her, I noticed she was holding unto her throat as if she felt my fists. I squeezed harder, harder; she was getting short of breath, reaching at her throat as if trying to release the grip. I held her throat tightly with my right hand while pulling her hair with my left. Just then the doctor who had led us into the ward rushed and attended to Viola, leading her out of the room. Her face had gone pale; a bluish colour had flushed over her skin. A rush of liquid raced pass me, I heard screaming and throbbing. My mother held her belly. "My water broke!" she yelled, trying to get over to the couch. Blood was now all over me, my feet could feel air.

A new doctor had come in to attend to her, it was Linda Wright. Something had grabbed hold of my feet. I heard screaming. A beating sound, almost like a tribal drum, it was her heartbeat still stifled. It was racing. It seemed like a well-orchestrated save. I wondered what that was, me gripping in anger and Viola feeling the effect of me grabbing her throat while still inside the womb. I felt pressure pushing me out while Linda was gently guiding my feet out. Slowly I felt myself easing out, I was being born. I felt my body getting hotter. I was out of her body, ou of the womb, free of the uterus. Linda rushed me over to somewhere- the vision ended. I was standing on the balcony with Nathaniel, Edith and Linda, sweat was pouring down my body, I felt hot, feverish. I had just seen my entire trimester, I saw myself born. That had to be the weirdest and most peculiar experience I ever had. I saw around me going dark, I felt weak I was falling to the ground. Darkness was all around.

*   *   *

I felt something touching me, my face. Cool water was pouring over me, soothingly. I felt a hand gently wiping my face with a sponge. My eyes were slowly opening. Edith was tenderly passing the sponge over my face. I heard a voice whisper, 'welcome back'. It was Edith, but her mouth hadn't moved. She was smiling, staring at me with a motherly look. I glanced around. Edith had turned gesturing for Nathaniel and Linda to come. We were inside the house and I was spread on a couch. I thought that I was maybe dreaming.

"Welcome back Shaun." Linda offered as she walked towards me.

"Did you know that she could talk?" I asked looking at Edith.

"Telepathically... yes, verbally... no." Nathaniel responded

"How long was I out?" I asked.

"Oh, just about two hours." Linda responded.

"I need to call Jimmy, see if he's okay."

I took my phone and dialled Jimmy, it rang out. I called the house phone and mummy answered. She told me that Jimmy was still fast asleep, he got up briefly and fell asleep. I was happy that he was getting rest, plus it gave me time to get home so it would not seem like I abandoned him. I was still a bit baffled by the experience Nathaniel had given me, confused. I controlled things by just thinking them, thinking what I wanted to happen. I had almost suffocated Viola, me... in the womb. I was seeing through people's eyes, feeling what they felt, manipulating their behaviour. As I thought about it, it seemed like he heard me.

"That's quite a gift you have there. Not only do you have telepathic abilities, there's the divination, aura reading, psychokinetic powers... you possess them all. I have never in all my years met someone so profound." Nathaniel said.

"I don't even know what to say. I'm not even sure exactly what just happened."

"Don't you worry son, with training, we can get this thing under control. I know your powers are intense and when you have unlocked your full potential, you will be even more of a force to be reckoned with. When situations get tough, your instincts will kick in. It's a part of you."

"So what is the significance of my birth?"

"Well... your situation is rare; it's something that doesn't usually happen. You went all three trimesters in the womb in a standing position... The significance is bigger than you and me. Most babies are in the proper foetal position, which is the head down, full utero."

"Shaun, what he is saying is that no matter if you were chosen, your birth... it's almost unheard of. None of the preceding were born that way, even if we were chosen, your situation, it's unusual... We all had normal births, full term and normal trimesters. There was nothing odd or remarkable about our prenatal or neonatal processes." Linda explained.

"Okay..." I responded still a bit bewildered by everything, "That makes perfect sense."

"Don't worry! When the time comes... you will surely have no questions. Our instincts kick in when needed, and our greatness shows under pressure. When the time is right, you will see what you are capable of." Nathaniel added.

"Well I think it's time we head back to Paradise. I will be back to visit soon. Get Shaun back to town."

"No problem sis! You're welcome anytime! You too Shaun, we're all family, so feel free." Nate assured. "It was great meeting you, an honour!"

"Thank you all so much." I responded, though I was still a bit puzzled, I felt at ease, I felt comfortable.

Nathaniel and Edith walked us out and accompanied us to the car. Linda reversed from the driveway and unto the dirt road. As we did, Edith and Nathaniel stood waving. I could hear Edith's voice calling out to us saying goodbye as we drove off. Something about her, though she couldn't speak, I heard her loudly. Her voice was so clear, as she spoke. It seemed like she had a lot to say. We made our way from Truth and Consequences, heading toward the Vérité Bridge. I couldn't stop thinking about everything. An information overload, I felt my head pounding, my temples throbbed from the pressure. At that moment I noticed a sign for the Vérité Bridge, only it didn't quite say Vérité on it. It said Les Conséquences. Les Conséquences Bridge was and on it 'Paradise Falls 10 miles'. We drove unto the bridge and as we did, the overhead sign read 'You are now leaving Pike Creek, we hope you enjoyed your stay' it was a nice gesture. A little lower down, I tried to make sense... Leaving Paradise Falls and going into Pike Creek the bridge was named La Vérité; entering Paradise Falls leaving Pike Creek the bridge was named Les Conséquences, one bridge but two names. I pondered I knew it was French but at the time it never occurred to me to translate... until that moment.

La Vérité meant the truth and Les Conséquences simply put was the consequences... Truth and Consequences. Each side had one half of the phrase. I remembered all the things Latricia said at the briefing, the things that everyone else had said. I wondered if anyone had ever taken notice. To me it seemed like Paradise Falls was referred to as the consequence, while Pike Creek was referred to as the truth... The lost town of Truth and Consequences was right there... the charms, the spells... that's why no one knew where it was. What was so special about Pike Creek about Truth and Consequences? Why did it have to be hidden?

I wanted to ask Linda but I remembered what Linda had said "In Paradise or anywhere inside of Consequences, one must be careful of what he or she says, 'for once it reaches the air, it reaches evil's ear'. The things that speak the loudest are those that bear no sound. The loudest sound anyone can hear is silence." The words kept playing over in my head. I heard Linda's voice answering me... 'Even the little things in life have great significance. At times we over think things and miss what was right before our eyes. Pike Creek or Truth and Consequences is where the truth lives, it's where lies come to light. Paradise Falls i a land of consequences, nothing is really as it seems, for what seems isn't always so simple'.

I tried to make sense of what she said. It all seemed like another parable to me. Nothing was direct; everything said was like a riddle. Growing up I was always taught that things should not be measured by their size to determine their worth, so that made sense to me, it's the thought that counts, but that referred to nice gestures by others... I guess it could be applied in any situation. Interpretation of things may be shaded by our own concepts and misconceptions or by our views of the world and hov things should be, these things that could influence our belief systems, who we are and who we turned out to be.

We got into Paradise at just around 1:25 p.m. that afternoon. It seemed like we had spent such a long time there, with all the visions and stuff, I guess me being passed out was what took the most out of the time we spent. She drove back to town hall where my car was parked and before leaving she reminded me that anytime I needed to contact anyone, all I had to do was reach out to them. I knew exactly what she meant. She smiled and waved as she left. I got to my car and drove home. When I got there Jimmy was still asleep. Mum had already prepared lunch so I decided to wake him up to eat.

"Oh man... good morning! I was out cold."

"I can see that." I laughed. "It's afternoon."

Jimmy looked at me surprised, "What time is it?"

"Well, it's like 2:12 now. I just thought I'd wake you up to get something to eat."

"Oh man, mom would never have let me sleep this late," he chuckled, "it's never going to do any good... it's what she says. It's great to be back in Paradise. It's so relaxing."

"Good day Jimmy!" Mum had walked in, "Shaun, finally you're back! Dad and I waited so we could all have lunch together. Since Jimmy's now up and you're back I'll go set the table. You guys be there in ten minutes."

"Yes auntie!" Jimmy answered.

"Okay mum, we'll be there in a bit."

I wanted to tell Jimmy about my trip to Pike Creek, Truth and Consequences but I knew I couldn't just tell him. I had to be extra careful where I spoke and what I let out, and since my new ability, I had to be careful of my thoughts as well. We went to the dining room where mum had started setting the table, we helped her get it done and sat down and waited for dad to watch the last few minutes of his cricket game. He came in a few moments later, his team had lost. I had no interest in cricket; to me it was a dull pastime. It was too long and seemed boring, I only thought of it as a more active version of golf... in my opinion.

We all sat down to dinner, "How was your day Jimmy?" Mom asked.

"I didn't see much of it, but it was great. Got some well needed rest, I haven't slept like that in ages."

"Sleep, you were practically selling the house! I heard you snoring from the back yard as I worked." Dad added teasingly.

"Uncle..." Jimmy said turning red, "I don't usually snore."

"I know, that's why I thought there was an auction going on..." Dad laugh as he spoke, "I had to come in and make sure no one had left with anything!" He laughed even louder.

"Oh dad, come on now." I tried to calm him down.

"Oh you mister, the day of that storm I wondered if the storm was confined only to the inside of our house."

I had riled him up. Shaking my head I said, "Isn't this a great lunch? Good job as always mum." trying to change the subject.

"Thank you, I figured it's Sunday and we could all have used some comfort food seeing all that has been happening."

"This is truly comfort food! I feel awake!" Jimmy added, with a mouthful.

"Where were you today Shaun?" Mom asked. We had managed to change the course of dad's jokes.

"I went over to Pike Creek..."

"Nice! The last time we went there you were about six years old. You were really sick and we took you to the hospital, private doctors and they all said they had no idea what the problem was. Then on our last visit to the hospital, a doctor approached us, Dr. Richards and he told us to go to Pike Creek to a Mrs. Edith." Mom said cheerfully.

"How is it that I don't remember any of this?"

"I remember that, I was scared. At times I didn't even want to go to school... I was afraid that I'd go one day and I'd come back and you'd be gone. I spent all my free time just sitting there with you, talking to you. I didn't want to lose my little brother." Jimmy said looking sad as he spoke.

"You were so sick, at times you'd be in a deep sleep for days and when you'd wake up you'd throw up weird stuff, like clear slime or clear green slime. It was scary. A lot of the time you were just in a trance." Mummy answered.

"Had we not taken you there, you maybe would not be here today. I never believed in bush doctors or things like that but whatever they did worked. I was always a sceptic until I realised that we might have been losing our only child. So we took you there and they did some things and gave you tea to drink and from there you just got better. They asked us to take you back to the hospital after three weeks and when we did they were shocked at the recovery you'd made. They couldn't even diagnose you or treat you and here three weeks later you're all well again." Dad had shed even more light on the events.

After dinner Jimmy and I headed upstairs. We hang out in my room for a bit playing video games and talking. I needed to find a way to tell Jimmy about my trip to Pike Creek, to tell him about all the things that had been happening and unfolding. He asked about Latricia and me and about our date. He joked that I'd never done anything so thoughtful with him, we laughed and joked about it and I insisted that I would. I brought up our dinner conversation; it was my first time hearing about that, about any of it. He explained to me that my parents didn't really talk about it much after I recovered and since I didn't have any recollection of that period, they thought it best to let it be. He didn't want to keep it from me, but he also didn't want to go against my parents' will. I understood what he was saying. He apologised, although I saw no reason for an apology, the situation was totally understandable. He only did what was right.

I remembered my trip to Pike Creek, and what I learned. If Jimmy was one of these things, an aura, I could surely speak to him without having to speak a word. I tried and at first I felt funny Jimmy never really told me anything about that although at times I felt like I heard his voice, I always thought maybe it was my imagination. I called out his name and heard nothing. He looked at me. I called his name again and he raised his eyebrow. I think he was hearing me. I called him again and he answered. My eyes opened wide and I heard him laugh. I asked whether he could hear me, he answered not only could he hear me, but he could also hear my conversation with myself. I started to speak to him casually, he told me to focus only on one thing and clear my mind. Then imagine him and myself alone in a dark silent place. It took some time, but it worked. I started telling him everything, piece by piece He didn't seem moved by any of the other stuff, he was amazed at me.

Jimmy started working at the station and we shared an office and became partners. He met all the staff including Latricia. We all hung out and at times Tessa came along with us. We spent the next few days hanging out and trying to get me more experienced with my telepathy. He also taught me some new things, things I didn't know I could do, I amazed myself. On our free time we'd learn a new ability after I had gotten comfortable enough with one he had started teaching me. We started playing tricks on people in the office, mainly those we were not particularly too keen about.

Chapter 16

This too Shall Come to Pass

It was Saturday night, the night before Halloween and Jimmy, Latricia, Tessa and I were going to Venice, a local nightclub in town. The place was crowded and the music was upbeat and lively, dancehall music, reggae, hip-hop, dance music. The deejay was not disappointing and the crowd was going crazy. Everyone was dressed up in their costumes and some looked so real and lifelike, I thought that a lot of effort was put into them. People were dressed up as witches, elves, trolls, ogres, vampires almost all creatures, including police, sexy strippers, angels and fairies. I was dressed up as a vampire myself and James decided to go as a zombie werewolf, Latricia was a mortician – a dead mortician and Tessa was a sexy seductress, or a siren. We stayed at the bar for a little just chatting and enjoying ourselves when Andrew Johnson walked in, dressed as Charlie Brown... it suited him well, his head was just the right size. There were four other jock type guys right behind him, well built. I assumed they were his goons. He made his way over to us, his goons right on his tail. Latricia and Tessa both looked most annoyed as he got closer. Tessa turned away from him avoiding his stare. She looked increasingly uncomfortable and Latricia looked furious. She stood up as he got closer as if ready for battle.

Jimmy nudged me, trying to get my attention; he had also noticed the changes and was staring directly at Andrew. Andrew and James had gone to school together and were in the same class for a few years. Jimmy and Andrew never got along, no one really got along with Andrew. He was known during that time as a bully, and he was always very slow like he had a mental disability... he was just really stupid- a jerk. He was mainly tolerated because of his parents. His mother was the principal of the secondary school and his father was the chief of police. When his father had passed away he was eighteen, his father died a tragic death, and he was found in pieces, shred to bits. His killer was never found and the case went cold because there was not enough evidence. Luckily for Andrew, his father had served more than fifteen years and he got accepted into the police force that same month his father passed. He never went through police training or academy, it seemed like he got the job only because his father was the police chief. He was promoted; it seemed based on family name.

"Hey family, how are you guys doing?" He said smugly with a sarcastic grin on his face. His friends laughed as if he had given a hilariously splendid joke... A joke the rest of us had missed.

"What are you doing here Andrew?" Latricia asked with a disgusted tone.

His friends ooed suggesting that she might have crossed the wrong path or maybe stepped on his toes.

"Is it a crime for me to be in a public place?" He asked as if taunting her. I started to get angry.

His friends laughed again, cheering him on as he kept on.

"There's nothing wrong with you being here, the problem is you coming around us! We do not want to have anything to do with you! I'd appreciate if you left my sister alone!" Latricia yelled, speaking loud enough over the music that the people around us heard her.

"I'm not bothering anyone. I'm just here enjoying my party. Aren't you guys having a blast? Like this music is just awesome." He was really beginning to get on my nerves, I didn't know what was happening but his taunting was getting to me. Nothing about him had changed; he was still a bully, just older.

We started to walk away, trying to get to another side of the club but Andrew and his bodyguards had blocked us in preventing us from getting away from them.

"Is there going to be a problem here?!" I said sternly stepping in between Latricia and Andrew.

His friends pushed me off, I got even angrier, I hated being touched. I did nothing I just let it go. They laughed and cheered him on as if he was doing something spectacular. "A problem? I don't see any of you here as a threat so I doubt there will be any problems. Let's not forget who I am. You feel me?" His arrogance was starting to show and I was getting increasingly angry.

"You won't see a threat, I never intended on being one, but I can guarantee you if you keep on doing what you're doing now, the problem will be solved, and that little line about knowing who you are... you're just a little punk to me, that same bully in high school, a scared little child taunting everyone else so he could feel better." A crowd had gathered around us as I spoke I didn't realise I was shouting and right in front his face with my hands playing in front of him. Jimmy had come pulling me back.

"Whoa! Slow down lil' bro. Just take it easy." He pulled me to the side, turning to Andrew he continued, "Hey um, bud we'd really appreciate if we can just enjoy our evening without an problems. We just came here to have a good time, we're not bothering anyone and we're not trying to get into anything but fun."

"Who the hell are you talking to? Who are you calling bud' You little punks better recognise who I am."

Jimmy was now angry, "I was only trying to diffuse a likely situation but you seem to be amped up and steaming huh? If you don't step off -bucky, they'll be wiping you off the floor with a sponge and a bucket!"

I found myself trying to pull Jimmy back, just then Andrew swung at him hitting him right in the nose, a sucker punch. Andy's boys had all seemed ready to attack and I knew then it was time to let go of Jimmy, because this was going to be a showdown. Jimmy's nose was bleeding from the punch and I saw that he was irate and fuming. He swung back with a right jab hitting Andrew straight in the temple. Andrew fell to the ground and everyone in the crowd cheered excitedly. I saw Andrew's buddies charging and I got even more upset. I felt my body getting hot, like my pressure was rising. I felt the room go dark, like everything had become a blur... everything except for Andrew and his buddies. The only people I could have seen at that moment were them. I rushed at them but I had thoughts in my head, I wanted them to feel pain, to suffer. I imagined one of them on fire, as I did it's like he was standing in an invisible fire pit. He started jumping and dancing around as if he was being scorched by flames that were not seen by anyone else but him. He was screaming and run towards the door. I noticed something about him; he looked like one of these dark figures. I looked around at the others and noticed they were all the same. I focused on the others and I felt my eyes burning into them, like something had taken control of me. I felt like I had completely blacked out.

When I looked again, I noticed they had all run off, heading for the exit. Latricia was looking at me awestruck and dumbfounded. Jimmy had stopped in place and just stood staring at me. Tessa was in the corner looking frightened, as if she'd seen a ghost. I wondered what happened. The three of them came to me and tried to calm me down. I noticed the security guards and bouncers were all standing around too, looking scared. Everyone looked terrified. I looked around trying to figure out what everyone was looking at. Then I realised they were looking at me. I didn't know what was so scary about what I had done. I didn't even understand why Andrew and his buddies went off running. Latricia, Jimmy and Tessa were leading me out of the club, holding me. As we left I saw blood on the floor. I thought it was from Jimmy's nose. Looking at the crowd I noticed that some of the costumes were not costumes at all. I could see them, real creatures staring at me with rage, like I'd done something to them.

How was no one else seeing this, and why were they escorting me from the club like a convict?

Voices started talking in my head all at once. Linda, Nathaniel, Anthony Hank, Father Monroe and Jimmy... Jimmy? Jimmy had telepathic abilities, and he knew how to use them. They were all speaking at once, they were saying that something was going on, something big... something bad. As we got outside I felt a change, the darkness seemed different... It seemed darker, heavier. It was now Sunday morning, October 31st. I saw a hen crossing the street heading toward the club with six chicks.

Nothing seemed unusual about that, but it was 1:00 a.m. and chickens were never out at that hour, but it still didn't strike me as odd. A vehicle was coming fast down the road, barrelling down as if there was no posted speed. As the car got close to the hen and her chicks, they stopped in the middle of its path. Just as the car got an inch from them, it started breaking up into tiny fragments like it had imploded. The pieces got finer as they spread they seemed to be dissolving. We stood in disbelief, almost frozen in our spots. Something was happening to the hen and her chickens; they were changing, changing into people. It happened so quickly but they all transformed. The hen was Lilith; she looked young, like she was in the visions. The other chickens were all in suit, Viola, Judith, Chief Tubbs, Alicia, Pearl and Amber.

They were all dressed in their black cloaks, they looked like corpses. Their skin was slimy and cracked, eyes flaming red and they were floating above the ground coming towards us. Others from the club had joined them, there seemed to be so many. I felt powerless. It was only Jimmy and me; I didn't see any way that we could have stood against them. They were an army and seemed prepared. I didn't know what they were capable of but from what I'd seen, the surveillance tapes from Peter's home invasion and in the visions or experiences with Nate and Linda, I knew they were forces to be reckoned with. Sparks of light and cracking sounds emerged from the club. It sounded like an electrical storm. Bright lights and surges of power almost like an electrical storm, the music stopped and screaming erupted as patrons came running from the exit doors. People were tripping as they tried to escape whatever was happening. Anthony Hank materialised along with some others dressed in black cloaks.

They were all next to Lilith and her posse. He waved his hand and Latricia and Tessa both froze in their place. I felt the need to defend us, Anthony had turned against us. The fury burned deep within me, I waved my hand and he flew back as if he had been struck forcefully by something huge. He knocked his back flying into a tree. I felt myself above the ground floating. My skin had turned glasslike, almost transparent... crystal like the woman from my vision. I felt heat surrounding me. I saw a glow emanating from me. I had changed into something. The reapers all looked at me, stunned. I looked and saw Jimmy was dressed in white, like the auras I had seen in the experiences. I heard Anthony Hank speaking directly to me, in my head.

"Good job Shaun, but next time go easy. I had to do it, I'm only trying to save them they're still alive, only in an unconscious state. They look petrified but they're not. This is a lot better than what one of the others would have done to them. I also don't want

Lilith or any of the others suspecting anything, at least not just yet."

I felt his emotions. I tried to read Latricia and Tessa... Hank was telling the truth. He was only trying to protect them. They were alive but frozen, frozen in place, frozen in time. I felt something squeezing at my neck, like someone was choking me. I looked over and saw that Lilith was coming closer to me. She had a hold on me, a firm grip at my throat. I felt myself losing breath.

"That's it master! Kill him!" Andrew's voice was shouting.

"Shut up you infidel! You babbling idiot! You almost compromised our plan!" she raised her left hand and I saw Andrew falling to the ground screaming. "I said don't do anything stupid. We were supposed to attack at 3:00. You had to do something stupid! You could have ruined everything. You will suffer for your sins. I will show you!"

Andrew rose above the ground going higher. His skin started falling off from under his cloak, she was skinning him alive. His flesh was exposed, bare and bleeding as his skin fell to the ground. He was engulfed with flames. Something flew and swoop him up, it looked like a huge winged dragon like creature, almost like a gargoyle. It swallowed him whole and disappeared. She had killed him; she had ruthlessly killed one of her own. It was so easy for her and she didn't even seem bothered in the least. She had just taken his life like it was a regular routine.

Pearl and Alicia both came at me, mercilessly.

"Finally I get to take my revenge on you. I should have killed you as a worthless child. You were just a disgusting powerless pipsqueak in my classroom!" Pearl shouted as she shot spurs at me, her spurs were boa constrictors. They wrapped around me while Lilith still had a grasp on my neck.

"You were weak and powerless then and now you're even more pathetic! Tonight we finish you!" Alicia added on firing her spurs at me, vultures emerged circling around above me then swooping down to attack me.

I felt a burning desire in me, with the snake wrapped tightly around me, squeezing forcefully I felt my insides burning with rage. The light radiated from me, it was blue and white. The snake shrieked and started to break up in fragments. I shot out stags of light out, they turned into white panthers and attacked the vultures Alicia shot at me. Lilith was still holding unto my neck, I felt her grip loosening just a little but not enough to break free. Nathaniel attacked Pearl, slashing her with five crystal claws on his right hand. She fell apart slowly. Six slices of what used to be her melted falling to the ground. Linda rushed at Pearl, turning into a phoenix. She flew swiftly but gracefully, clawing Alicia's mouth open with her claws. Alicia tried to hold Linda but the flames coming from her burned Alicia. Linda dropped five feathers from her tail into Alicia's mouth and flew away. Alicia screamed in pain and agony. Her eyes shout out blue light, like the headlights of a car. Then flames cut through her insides bursting through her flesh and cutting through her skin. As she screamed, the flames devoured her and she became a charred fragment, a coal statue and fell to the road breaking into pieces. Lilith was even more crossed. She looked disappointedly at her fallen soldiers.

Jimmy had sent out bright white lights at her. The rest of her reapers started to fight back. I used this time of distraction to fight back. I grabbed hold of the grip around my neck and opened my fist. Lilith went crashing into a car that was driving off, disabling it. The reapers were coming at us taking revenge for their master. Jimmy shot up blue and red sparks into the sky. I remembered Emila sending those out. Just as he had done that, bright flashes of white light emerged and from them appeared Edith, Father Monroe and Cynthia. Anthony Hank was no longer wearing a black cloak; he was in white like us, those of the light. The battle ensued getting more violent. Lilith looked disgusted as she looked at Anthony. She looked at him the same as she did Andrew. She wanted him dead. Father Monroe flew through the air attacking her before she got a chance to attack Hank. Viola went after him relentlessly, sending violent spurs at him, snakes and dragons rushed at him. Edith teleported and appeared just behind Father Monroe facing the spurs her mouth opened wide and she swallowed the spurs. Her eyes glowed brightly; they went black with a white glow. She rushed at Viola.

"I've been waiting for this moment all my life! You killed my mother and now you will pay!" Edith spoke, for the first time she spoke. She disappeared and appeared in front of Viola, directly at her face. She stretched out her hands and grew long crystal claws and sent her right hand slashing Viola's face, jabbing her left hand into Viola's neck. A black gooey liquid slowly oozed out, Viola's eyes went white, white veins glowed through her cloak. I saw sparks of white light emitting from Edith as she latched onto Viola. More of the liquid gushed out; it started turning a greyish white glowing colour. Viola screamed as if possessed. A bright glow surrounded them and Viola disappeared with a loud cracking sound. A coin fell in the spot where she was.

Lilith was wailing, she started elevating higher above the ground. Electrical wires broke as she went up, and surges of electricity went into her. She was getting stronger, absorbing the energy. Her cloak seemed to come to life, it seemed animated and one of the pleats like an octopus's tentacle reached and grabbed Father Monroe wrapping around him. Hank moved forward trying to save Father Monroe and roots shot out from the ground spooling around him like thread and pulling him into the ground. I didn't know what to do. I noticed that I had gone up higher above the ground, moving towards Lilith, I was rushing at her with all my might. My hands got sharp almost like diamond cuts and I lunged at her, going for her heart. Linda and Nate were right behind me. As we neared her, from below I noticed skeletons emerging from the ground. She had awakened an army, an army of the dead. We were outnumbered and it seemed like our powers were not enough to win.

Lilith slowly floated toward us, dark purple rays of light surrounded her, it seemed like there was a lightning storm consuming her. Lights in the vicinity went out and drew to her as she seemed to be growing stronger. She came at us forcefully, Father Monroe still firm in her grip. Jimmy disappeared from the spot where he was and he appeared in the air where Father Monroe was, he grabbed onto him and teleported. Jimmy seemed well versed, like he knew what he was doing. The army of the dead was attacking everyone down below, all the club goers and pedestrians. Lilith's reapers were also attacking, sucking the life out of their victims after they had shot them with spurs, leaving behind mummified corpses in their wake.

Lilith, Chief Tubbs and the others attacked us ruthlessly. Edith climbed into Chief Tubbs's mouth, his flesh cracked like the ground in a desert or like a swamp during a drought. Through the cracks bright light flashed like that of a camera and a spray of oozing black and greyish green liquid fell like rain, a coin glistene as it fell into the bushes below. Amber went after Edith, she looke like a witch as she flew across the sky. She changed into a water demon, and Edith changed into a siren, letting out a loud wailing shriek. The sound was deafening. Amber called out and the pipes below broke open and water flowed toward her, and she absorbed all the moisture from the air. She sent barrelling waves of water at Edith, knocking her out of balance. Edith fell to the ground and th army of dead attacked her. Amber laughed and smiled proudly. Nate struck her, a sharp jab through her heart, his hand opened in her body taking the exact shape. The light from him glowed beneath her skin as she expanded, her flesh stretched and she grew until she couldn't anymore. She slowly changed back into herself as soon as the transformation was complete; she exploded throwing pieces of her all over. Another coin fell to the ground.

A loud wailing sound came from below and it was Edith breaking through, still in her siren transformation. Her wails broke through the walls of the undead that had buried her. Windows shattered all around as her wails spread. A bright beam of light appeared behind Lilith, and another in front of her. The light before her was Jimmy, but there was something else there with him. The figure slowly materialised, she looked almost like the silver surfer and as she changed I noticed it was Emila. She rushed and lunged at Lilith, it was a heated battle. The light behind her was Xavier. Xavier disappeared and appeared in splinters of light next to Hank and disappeared with him. He reappeared where Edith lay, almost immobile, blood was all over her, held unto her and they both disappeared. Lilith knocked Nate and Linda sending them billowing to the ground. Nate crashed through the ground like a comet and Linda landed in the trees leaving a path of broken trees and a clearing where she landed. Lilith's army of the dead all grew boned wings and took flight.

Epilogue

Time Never Stops

They looked more ferocious. Demons started coming from everywhere. Again it seemed we were powerless, outnumbered by the minions, by the soldiers of darkness. Xavier returned right above Lilith, a shiny silvery sword in his hand, disappearing and reappearing cutting all the tentacles that came from her. Just as he cut the last one, she conjured a spartacum and sent it at him. The demon grew as it got closer to him. It started to look more lively more powerful and it roared as it moved. With the roaring were wails, screeching sounds and shrieks. Its wings flapped valiantly, swooping down on him breathing fire from its nose. Xavier put up a light shield that repelled the flames. The spartacum flew up into the sky beyond the clouds and out of sight. I went towards Lilith and wrapped my hand around her neck. We both went plummeting to the ground, rolling over as we fell. She placed me beneath her and I crashed into the ground.

She put both her hands around my neck, grasping firmly. I pulled my arm over my head getting space to get a good accurate swing. I balled my hand to a fist and launched it at her, knocking her across her right temple. She went soaring forcefully knocking into a tree breaking it down. As I tried getting up I was rushed by the winged demons, their powers were dark and mysterious. They drained the life from you, drained all warm emotions, all warm thoughts and if weak willed they'd consume all of you leaving only darkness. They planted thoughts in my head making me question my beliefs, my faith. Their way was deception and they tried profusely. As they did I could feel myself going cold. My crystal like form started going dark. At that very moment I saw a dark flash of purple lightning and the demon of death appeared, slowly hovering towards me. It was now 3:00 a.m. As it moved darkness consumed everything it passed, everything went dark. It had spread its wings, its pitch black eyes stared directly into mine, burning into my soul. All the other demons had released their grip and started returning to the ground.

Linda, Nate, Emila and Xavier all came to a standstill, as if frozen in time. The only thing that moved was the darkness. I saw my deepest darkest fears; the shadows were slowly eating up at my insides. I felt all my happy memories slipping away from me. Flashes of my pain and anguish were all I could see, the only happy emotions I felt were murky and obscure, fading slowly. Surges of dark emotions, dull and sinister were flowing through me. I looked at myself and the darkness was slowly creeping up my body. I felt like a shadow, barren, desolate and derelict. My heart started to feel heavy, as if it was turning to stone. It got closer to me, proudly stretching it wings, wings that just resembled an exoskeleton. Time had stood still; everything had frozen except for it and me. I tried to get up, but my body was slowly growing rigid. It spoke to me, directly to my soul. I felt my insides quiver, my body trembled. My stone limbs became heavier. A little light came from my head and chest area.

It was the only thing visible now in the darkness. Everything else had disappeared. It was beckoning me to become one with the darkness, it promised me all my desires. It offered me all my dreams. All I had to do was give my soul, and the world would be mine. I knew that if I chose this, I'd be damned to an eternity of darkness. There would be no warmth and I would never be satisfied. The world would not be enough to please me, as greed and dark and lustful desires would be all I knew. The pain of others would be my cornerstone; my satisfaction would come from suffering. I tried to fight it off but it was persistent. It started blaming me for the death of my grandparents, planting thoughts and memories in my head that never took place.

I started to believe them. I saw my best friend drowning again, I had blocked that memory. I felt it was my fault that he had drowned because I didn't do enough that day to stop him from going to the river. I was only eleven years old. He had made up his mind. I felt something bad coming his way. I begged and pleaded with him not to go, but his other friends insisted that he went. I stayed home looking out for them to return, but hours passed and they never showed. I remembered hearing sirens, and people screaming loudly. My neighbours came calling me telling me that Calvin had drowned. I didn't believe, I thought it was a joke. Something deep within me told me that he was gone. I hoped for the best, I prayed but nothing. The demon was using this to turn against what I knew was right. It urged me to disown God, and serve him as master. It promised that I could bring my best friend back to life and take away all the pain.

I started to believe, but I still felt the darkness, there was no hope, no happiness, no joy, only sorrow, burdens and dark thoughts. I tried and tried to fight it, fighting his lies, but the more I did, the harder he tried and the greater his offers became. A light started to emerge, I tried to pray, and as I mentioned God the demon got angrier. I started to say the Lord's Prayer, and I felt the demon grasping at my heart. Gripping firmly unto it, my heartbeat slowed. The more I prayed, the angrier it got, it became more violent. I started to remember what happened to Peter, what happened to all the others and I felt my anger strengthening me. The light started becoming brighter; something started manifesting in the middle of the light. The demon had seemed to become more furious, the light became brighter and slowly I saw something materialising. I heard a voice, a familiar voice speaking to me, telling me not to give up. I felt strength coming to me and as the voice spoke the more powerful I started to feel.

The more I felt the brighter the light became. More and more the manifestation started to take form. An outline stood in the light. It spoke to me, telling me about all that life had to offer, the good things I had: my family, my friends... my life. I saw Calvin appearing. I felt weak. His voice started speaking more sternly to me, convincing me that it wasn't my fault. It told me I did all that I could, but it was his time to go, it was his calling and it was nobody's fault. Then he changed into somebody else, my grandfather was standing there, just as I remembered him when he was alive. Though he was old he was tall, energetic, strong and youthful. He looked pleasant and smiled at me, he reminded me of all that I had, all my loved ones and all the things I loved to do. Everyone that I loved who had passed away had appeared to me. I felt my strength returning, the light went through my body.

The demon was still strong, I felt him inside of me as I tried to stand. I managed to get up and I was now face to face with death, with darkness. I remembered Lilith killing Andrew, and attacking my friends. She tried to kill me, how could I possibly serve a master who wished me dead? I felt my rage fuelling me, anger was building up. As I thought, I got more livid, my anger had become my passion. I needed to fend off this demon, I needed to stand up to it, and I needed to face my fears. Nothing in life was worth me giving up my soul, my freewill, my freedom. All the riches in the world meant nothing to me when I considered all the other things I had, all the friendships, all of my family, all of my happy memories. Nothing that the demon was offering me would be worth anything in death, for without my soul I'd be dead.

A spark of light struck in front of me, between the demon and I. It went to the ground and started building from the ground up. It was Samira; she had come to our rescue. With a wave of her hands, the demon loosened its hold completely. She grabbed it and they both disappeared; as they did it seemed like time started moving again. I flew to the sky from the ground where I stood, attacking Lilith, driving my hand through her heart. Deafening screams and dark light shot out from her mouth. Her screams had sent the others tumbling to the ground. All the other demons and her servants vanished in wisps of smoke. Lilith looked at me, her eyes turning hollow. Then she disappeared and her voice echoed as the light returned. All she said was it was not the end, but the beginning and victory would be hers.

*   *   *

According to history and what we know, the world has become a complicated place. In reality, the world has always been a complicated place; things just change with time to blend in with the situation. Many things in order to be considered a fact or truth need to be believable, credible, intriguing, interesting, and also logical. If one looks beyond what is presented to them, they might see things that they didn't previously. Some stories are told to suit the teller or the crowd. Therefore; you'd find that by searching for more evidence, information, for other versions or accounts, some things in the story may be the same, while others are based on the beliefs of others, on their emotions and fears or even on their own lives. Always satisfy your thirst for more knowledge, never leave questions unanswered.

With every story that is told, the original can never be perfectly duplicated unless it is recorded as it happens and unfolds. Retelling of that same story can change the slightest detail, rendering the story unsound. Even an overlook of the slightest detail can make a huge difference, especially if the tone has changed. Changing something that is already great is not a problem; the problem begins when one person decides that change must be made and totally destroys something that was perfect. The best change one can make is improvement.

Life, the simple yet complicated cycle; it lives then it dies to start all over again. All life starts the same; it is thought of, planned, produced, created and introduced into the universe, into its world. Well versed and choreographed. The rules of this cycle remain the same throughout time. The actors may change and be replaced, but the roles, plot and story stay the same... well relatively. Scenes may change here and there and from time to time there might be some impromptu acting, but the storyline is still the same. With change comes differences, and differences are in part a comparison of two or more things: a comparison shows not only the differences but the similarities.

Though many people turn down the mere thought of the existence of things paranormal, there are many who still firmly believe in most of the so called "imaginations running wild" as being reality. Many people believe that paranormal things exist; things like aliens, the Bermuda Triangle, and even ghosts just to name a few. Even professionals and science has not answered many of these questions, some agree that there is a great possibility that many of these things exist, and would be willing to give accounts off the records, which leads to the conclusion that most people are too embarrassed to admit that they believe in "the paranormal". Most people even think it to be a disease... If that's the case it's a wide spread epidemic and many are infected. Today most of these things have been regarded as fake, irrelevant, and even stupid, but who is to determine their existence or nonexistence... who is to prove the sceptics and doubters wrong, who is to plead the case of the believers? Maybe an open mind over a narrow mind would make a whole difference, but then again… You never really know.

Everything in life has significance, it may not be apparent at that very moment, or it may not matter to you, but to someone else it means so much more than you could fathom. Life at times may hand us things that are greater than us, or beyond our understanding. Never shy away from a task. Attempt to understand it, look at it from all different perspectives, even ways that may seem ridiculous. At times it's the simplest explanation that is usually the answer. If something is more than we understand... remember it's not too much for us to try. We are never given anything more than we can handle. Times may be tough, but you are stronger than any situation you are faced with.

Never be discouraged and never be afraid. Challenge yourself, for what may seem like a mountain from a valley, will seem like a valley from a mountain. Nothing in life that is a material thing is worth dying for, nor is it ever worth taking the life of another. Greed leads to many things, including losing one's self. Gaining all the riches in the world and losing your soul, losing yourself, losing life, is only a loss. At the end of it all, death is only the beginning, for who knows what comes after death. All we can answer is what comes after life. Time never stops, it doesn't pause or replay. All of it is continuous and consistent, though many things may change, time never does.

In everything you do remember that we are all human, none of us perfect or all pure. Treat your neighbour as yourself, for many times what we do in life always comes back to us whether directly or indirectly. Something that affects our loved ones or even strangers can also affect us greatly. Never treat anyone as less than an equal, never act like you are more than anyone else. We are all made up of the same things and when we die we will all become the same thing, unidentifiable, unrecognisable by others, our accomplishments, our riches and achievements won't be seen by looking at our remains, and they can never tell our whole story.

Made in the USA
Middletown, DE
14 October 2023

40770191R00123